UNHAPPILY
EVER AFTER

A COLLECTION OF
UNFORTUNATE FOLK TALES

T. T. PHILLIPS

First published 2025

The History Press
97 St George's Place, Cheltenham,
Gloucestershire, GL50 3QB
www.thehistorypress.co.uk

British Library Cataloguing in Publication Data.
A catalogue record for this book is available from the British Library.

ISBN 978 1 83705 005 5

Typesetting and origination by The History Press
Printed and bound in Great Britain by TJ Books, Padstow, Cornwall.

The History Press proudly supports
Trees for Life
www.treesforlife.org.uk

EU Authorised Representative: Easy Access System Europe
Mustamäe tee 50, 10621 Tallinn, Estonia
gpst.request@easproject.com

CONTENTS

FOREWORD

Thank you for buying my book. This is the third book I have had the honour of writing for The History Press and a bit of a departure from my previous format. My first two books were aimed at children, being collections of folk tales, rewritten for that audience. My background as a primary school teacher and the last sixteen years as a professional storyteller have stood me in good stead to write challenging and fun stories for this age group – that have also been enjoyed just as much by adult readers – but, with this book, I wanted very much to stretch myself.

Since I was a child, I have always had a fascination with traditional stories and folklore, and I found the ones that always stayed with me the most were those with unhappy endings. I quickly got bored with the Disneyfied cliché of 'happily ever after', so these stories, in which the main characters don't necessarily get all they hoped for and desired, spoke to me. They seemed to be a more fitting reflection on real life and – as I hit my teenage years and started to encounter exclusion and bullying, like many of us do – I found solace in the fact that even these folk tale characters couldn't get it right all of the time.

The most influential of all those stories I heard as a child was one that features in this book, *The Soldier and Death.*

I first encountered this story on television as a child thanks to Jim Henson's fantastic '80s series *The StoryTeller*. This story of bravery, cunning, and derring-do that explained why death is so important in this world, but also gave a sombre end with no happy ending for the soldier (spoilers, sorry), hit me for six. I have since revisited it many times, revelling in the marvellous performance by the late John Hurt, and the brilliant puppet designs by Jim Henson's Creature Workshop. This was also the first story I told in my storytelling career at a storytelling group in Nottingham. I told stories to my class as a teacher, but this was my first time telling in front of an audience of adults, so it holds that special place in my heart.

Throughout my career as a storyteller, I have collected many traditional tales with unhappy endings and have lived with them in my head, going around and around, forever finding new meaning depending on when and where I have told them. After a family holiday one year I began to write down my version of the first story of this book, *The Fisherman and the Selkie*. This was a story I first came across on my teacher training back in the mid-2000s, and have loved ever since. The recent trip to the Norfolk coastline set my mind racing. I was somewhat obsessed with pirates, sea shanties and nautical stories for a while before I put fingers to keyboard and began writing this story down. It was originally planned to be part of a book telling traditional seaside folk stories intertwined with my lifelong obsession with the coast, having been born and raised in the most landlocked county in Britain, Leicestershire. The call of the sea has always been strong within me, driven by family holidays as a child to the beautiful Pembrokeshire coastline.

I soon realised I would have a problem getting this book into print through The History Press as they like their folk tale book authors to have a connection to the tales they write. For instance, I wrote *Leicestershire Folk Tales for Children* and am, myself, Leicestershire born and raised, and followed up by writing *Forest Folk Tales for Children* whilst running a museum and country park at the heart of the National Forest. So, I began repurposing the book. I wanted to write folk tales in a more immersive and expansive way. I have been trying to write a middle school fantasy novel for many years and enjoy a longer form of storytelling – something you can't really do with traditional folk tale books. The stories tend to be shorter and more to the point. So, I broached the idea to the publishers, who were somewhat hesitant at first. I explained the premise again and settled on the theme of 'unhappily ever after' before they decided to give it a shot.

Since then, I have embarked on an eight-month mission to write this book. Despite missing the deadline by a few weeks, thanks to a rather enjoyable Christmas, I have completed it and really hope you enjoy reading these stories as much as I've enjoyed writing them. I have tried to challenge myself by writing each one in a different style, from traditional storytelling to a pastiche of nineteenth-century Gothic horror to trying to channel the wonderful writing style of one of my all-time favourite writers: the late, great Terry Pratchett. As any writer will tell you, they never feel their work is perfect and there are always things they would like to change, as is the case for me with this, but this is what I am unleashing on the world, and I hope you are kind with it. Writing anything and putting it out to the world is scary, wondering if people will like it, what the reviews will be like, whether it will sell well. The joy of writing is soon forgotten and replaced by worry, much like having a child and watching them finally go out on their own. All

I ask is that if you read this book and enjoy it, please write a review wherever you bought it from to let others know this book is worth their time and money and, in the process, support small authors like me. Then, go and check out the other folk tale books from The History Press, all written by storytellers like myself.

For those looking for a reference section, I have toyed with the idea of this. However, while I have referenced sources and people where I can, these stories have become ingrained within me, and I would struggle to cite all the places I have found versions of them. My memory is just not that good. Keep the stories with you and enjoy finding the different versions of each out there in the wild, being told, captured in a book, or turned into a film or TV series. The influence of these stories is far and wide and far outstrips any reference list I could write.

For reading to the end of this waffle you are amazing, and I thank you. I want to also thank my long-suffering wife. As a secondary school English teacher, she is always my first port of call and my proofreader. I couldn't have done this without you, Sam, thank you.

Anyway, enough with the foreword, let's get into it and hear about those unfortunate folk in those stories that all end with an 'unhappily ever after'.

THE FISHERMAN AND THE SELKIE

This title story to this folk tale collection is very old. It was one of the first I heard during my career as a teacher, with a simplified version being used as a text in a traditional tales block of work. I was struck straight away by the ending and loved the nods to far more adult themes. Since then, I have tracked the story down and read and heard many different versions, but each time the central theme was the same. The story revolves around a theme of coercion and control on a very subtle basis, asking the question of whether this is ever justified, even if the outcome is a happy one.

Selkies are mythical folkloric creatures found in Scottish and Scandinavian cultures. These are gentle creatures of the deep, not to be confused with their more vicious, malicious cousins, the finn folke. They are also closely related to their more famous cousins that dwell in the warmer seas to the south, the mermaids – but more about those in a later story.

Throughout this book, I have tried to change my writing style to give each one a different feel. For this first story, I found it only fitting to use a descriptive, atmospheric tone throughout. The rugged setting of this story seemed to fit with this style. Although I never explicitly tell the reader the location for this, leaving it purposefully vague, I aimed to paint a picture of a place that people may recognise from the landscape, the trades, the food and drink and the weather. I also used traditional names from the setting. The names themselves all have meanings that reflect the character. However, the main character, the fisherman, is left nameless on purpose, giving the reader a chance to place themselves in his shoes and decide themselves if his actions and motives were justified.

He lived alone, just him and the waves, changing with the seasons. The winter brought the anger and the wrath, the summer the contentment. The fisherman led a simple life, but a mostly happy one. His cottage sat two miles from the nearest port, clinging like a limpet to the cliff. The whitewashed walls guarded the fisherman from all the sea could throw at him whilst he hid inside them. Nets hung by the cottage in the postage-stamp walled garden, carefully placed stone encircling the ledge that the fisherman's world stood upon.

When the tide was against him, he sat and mended his nets, repairing holes from the rocks that grasped at them deep below the North Sea. But he preferred to be out there, out on the rise and fall, nothing but wood between him and the endless cold depths teeming with life and the great unknown. It was salt water that ran through his veins, not blood, topped up by whisky of an evening to help him sleep, for the land was too still and he craved the sway of the waves, the unbalance that drink brought to him.

He hadn't chosen the solitary life; it crept upon him like fungal growth on a soldier's damp foot. He didn't want this single life, but this is the life he now had, and he had accepted it. Besides, he had not the time to worry about a wife or a family. The sea was his mistress. If he was not fishing or mending nets, he was sorting his catch and taking it to the port to sell. The fisherman's catches were renowned for being the best around. He could read the sea better than any man and knew where the best fish were hiding. He would sort the wheat from the chaff, keeping the smaller fish – those he had not let free on the water – for himself. These, along with the bounty he foraged from the land's border with the sea – the mussels, whelks, seaweeds, and samphire, to name but a few – kept him well-fed. The rest of the catch brought him a handsome return, which he would then put back into the boat, to the repairs, to the fishing nets and his cliffside safe haven.

It was late spring. The sea had turned from its angry winter brown to its settled springtime green. The fisherman had enjoyed a rare night on land due to the turning of the tide, the unfinished net repairs, and an extended day at market selling a particularly large haul from the now-calmer waters. His head had hit the pillow after the whisky made it dance, and he slept a dreamless sleep. The moon was bright and fat and round that night, its silver light bathing the shoreline, showing the secret nooks and crags to whoever was looking, casting long shadows across the rocky beach below. The fisherman never had need for curtains. Those bits of cloth delayed you from rising in the morning. If the sun was up, so too should you be, he thought, for it was rude to not greet the sun in the morning. It was the least you could do for it. However, this night, as the sun was still very much in bed and the moon was very much out and in charge, the light it reflected from its celestial neighbour was so bright it roused the fisherman, his eyes believing it was the turning of the night and the breaking of the dawn. When he peered out the window to see it was just the sleeping satellite staring down at him, he looked at the clock that ticked its tock on the wall opposite his bed. It told him it was the early hours of morning. It was too late to go back to sleep, he thought, for the sun was but a few hours from its return and, once he had woken, he was seldom able to return to his slumber. He put the kettle on – what else was there to do?

As he stood on the stone threshold of his cottage, brew in hand, he breathed in the salt air and marvelled at the warmth of the coming morning. He closed his eyes and smiled at the promise of summer. It was then, with the absence of sight heightening his senses, he heard the music. Pipes – ancient pipes, the type his ancestors played – drifted over the warm breath of the night and roused within him a long-buried pride. He opened his eyes and looked down to the bay in which his boat was moored, and was greeted by a most unusual sight. On one rock sat the shape of a person, playing the pipes whilst, in front of them, a group of people danced. Their hair was as black as coal and flowed through the air behind them like the waves of the sea. The moonlight bounced off their plump, pale skin and, even from that height, the fisherman could tell these were all women, with curves that could drive a man to madness. Although he had come to terms with being alone, it did not mean his urges had left him entirely, and the fisherman found his feet carrying him down the well-trodden path towards the bay below.

Once there, the fisherman moved like a shadow. No noise came from his feet, his form flowing from rock to rock, getting ever closer to the piper and her dancers. When he found the perfect place to spy upon the delectable sight before him, he froze and drank in the vision of beauty. The women span on tiptoes, twirling light as a feather cast from a gull's wing in a strong breeze. Their hair was always flowing, always following, tracing their movements in the silver lunar light. It was then, several reels in, that the fisherman caught sight of them: the seal skins. They lay cast upon the rock beside the piper, silky smooth and soft with downy fur. His eyes flitted between the skins and the dancers, and a memory began to resurface, as a long-forgotten wreck is revealed during a neap tide.

He sat on his mother's knee; the smell of salt and fish guts ever present but somehow infinitely comforting. His head sank onto his mother's ample chest, which muffled the wind and rain outside that battered that very same cottage he lived in now. His mother's heartbeat pounded through her ribs, her voice reverberating through her very being, and the boy listened and the boy learnt. He learnt of the ways of the sea. Not the ways his father taught him, but the hidden ways, and of the people and the creatures the fisherman don't see but know they are there.

'There be several types of people that call the depths their home, my boy,' the fisherman's mother explained in a soft, loving voice. 'There are, of course, the mermaids... and mermen, of course! These creatures look as us humans do, from their heads to their middles, by which point their skin gives way to the most beautiful, delicate scales that cover a large tail. They live many leagues away where the water is warmer all the year-round.'

The boy nestled in closer, listening to every word. 'Then there are the finn folk. Beware the finn folk, me lad, for they will do thee harm sooner than look at ye! Mermaids may sing to ye, lure ye to the rocks – but not all of them, only those scorned by men. Nay, the finn folk does'nae care for how good a man's heart be, they will drag ye down to the depths and force the air from ye lungs with the sea water just for the hell of it!'

His mother's voice spoke with a wisdom of ages, the stories and knowledge passed from folk to folk through the tales they told. This was magic; a strong kind of magic that could hold fast even the most restless of men or women and drive home even the harshest of truths, and all would listen.

'And then there be the selkies, me boy.' Her voice softened now after the harsh tones she used to drive home the fear you must feel of the finn folk. 'Yes, the selkies. These are beautiful creatures that live just off our coasts. You have spied them many times before but not realised.'

The boy's young ears pricked up. Had he really seen some of the fae folk of the ocean and not known about it?

'They look as all can see to be seals, common or garden seals, their heads bobbing gently above the waves, watching the land folk go about their business. But–' the fisherman's mothers voice lowered, '–these are no ordinary seals! For when the moon is bright and full, the women of the group come to shore, shed their seal skins and dance in the silver moonlight all night long.'

The fisherman's young mind spun. Could this be possible?

'They cast off their skins, but put them back on and return to the sea before dawn. Without them,' explained his mother, 'they cannae withstand the cold of the depths, and would be forever stranded on shore.'

It was then, whilst the fisherman was half-drowned in thought, that she caught his eye. The woman with the green eyes; green like the sea, and twice as deep. From the shadows he saw her, lighter on her feet than all of them and twice as beautiful. The fisherman fell instantly in love. It was such a cliché, he would tell you that himself, something reserved for legends and old fishwives' stories. But there he was, tumbling head-over-heels for a woman he had only just seen, had never spoken to, and who did not even know he existed. The fisherman had to have her for his own, to hold her, to lay with her and be whole with her.

He had tried to court a woman before, but respectable young women are hard to find in small fishing ports, for they tend to move away to work when they are able. Occasionally the fisherman would stay late after the market to have an ale or five at the tavern. He would never have to buy himself a drink. The locals knew him well and thought he undersold his fish, so they were happy to repay him with a pint or two. He would hope that a young woman might happen upon the tavern, and he may begin talking to her, with one thing leading to another, but the only woman he found in that bar was the landlady. She, although bright and bubbly on the outside, was a tumultuous bubbling inferno below the surface, ready to crack together the heads of anyone who stepped out of line or simply looked at her ample chest in the wrong way. What way was the wrong way, you may ask? Suffice to say, any way seemed to be the wrong way, so customers preferred looking directly at their own feet rather than her, in case they were mistook to have had a mis-look. Needless to say, the visual of feminine loveliness before him now was several oceans away from what he was used to.

Visions of the life he could have raced through the fisherman's mind. A life of contentment, of warmth, of someone waiting for him on those long, wet, hard trips at sea, waiting with the fire blazing and a fresh-cooked meal waiting for him, of the warmth of a body next to him at night, of the gentle embrace of the woman he loved and of nights of passion. This merged into thoughts of children. He'd never wanted children; never seen the point until now. He imagined what his children with this selkie woman would look like. The dark hair. Would they have her green eyes or his brown? Would they share his love of the sea? Would they be tall or short, lively or thoughtful, boys or girls, or a mix? '*What, multiple children?*' he thought. This all came like a tidal wave washing away his sanity and, in that moment of blindness, he found himself creeping forward between the rocks, to the feet of the piper and the collection of seal skins.

Behind the piper he hid, the skins in reach. In the shadowy darkness he carefully looked over the skins. The one nearest to him, as luck would have it, shared a dashing white streak down it with the vision of beauty he had fallen for. Her white streak morphed in and out of her jet-black hair as she danced, a streak kissed by the moon itself. That was her seal skin. He felt it in his bones. Out reached his hand, creeping over the rock, and it fell upon the soft skin, his fingers flowing through the down. Back he dragged it, any noise drowned out by the melancholy drone of the pipes. He slipped away then, back amongst the rocks he knew so well. Finding a hidden place beyond the high tide line, he pushed the skin within, placing a large stone over the entrance. The skin was hidden, was safe, was his.

He then crept back to the path that led from the cottage to where the selkies danced, before rising up and walking towards them as though walking to the inn at the port. The piper ceased abruptly, the drone not getting the message to stop for several seconds. The dancing stopped. For a brief moment, the group of naked women froze and looked upon the fisherman in horror before they scrambled for their seal skins, slipping them on as we slip on socks, and launched themselves, on their bellies, in seal form, towards the safety of the sea. All of them, the piper, too... all except one. The fisherman was right. He had hidden the right skin. The distraught selkie scratched around on her hands and knees where the skins had been, desperately seeking hers, glancing back over her shoulder, aware of the fisherman approaching ever closer.

'Do you need help?' offered the fisherman, a cracked, weathered, but kindly smile on his face.

The selkie spoke, a broken speech, stuttered and slow. 'My skin. My skin, was here, now gone. Help find my skin.' All the time she kept searching, looking back and forth from the fisherman to the rocks and back.

The fisherman's eyes caught the selkie's and he smiled. 'Here, take my hand. We will look for it together. I understand.'

The selkie placed her delicate, soft trust in his outstretched hand and he led her down amongst the rocks to search. After some time, the selkie had still not found her skin. Now the moon was returning to its daytime home below the horizon and the sun had begun its steady march towards the horizon of the land. The black of the night sky had turned to dusty grey, and dawn was announcing itself to the world.

'I must go, go in sea, family, family!' The selkie pointed to the ocean, vast and endless, cold and wild, and the fisherman understood but said not a word about her skin. 'No skin, no in water, cold.'

'Come with me,' replied the fisherman, taking her hand once more. 'Come back to my house. The fire is burning. It is warm and I have clothes for you to wear.'

'What clothes?' Confusion crept across the selkie's face. Her seal skin was her clothes. She needed not the bits of cloth humans on the land needed to stay warm, so knew not of clothes.

'Come, come, I will show you.' The fisherman led the naked woman carefully up the cliff path to his cottage. They entered the door and, quickly, the fisherman lifted a blanket off a chair and wrapped it around the selkie's slim, bare figure, covering her skin for the first time with something other than her seal skin. It was scratchy and soft, warm and drafty, all at the same time. It wasn't the comfort and safety of her skin, but it was calming and comforting.

'Thank you,' she said softly.

The fisherman sat her down on the chair the blanket came from, in front of the fire, before stoking the ash to expose the embers. He placed some more logs upon them and bellowed air to the heart of the heat, causing flames to start licking up the chimney. The selkie's eyes grew wide with astonishment and wonder.

'What that?' Her voice was full of childlike wonder at the magic of the fire in front of her. She then felt the warmth on her exposed legs, creeping up, wrapping her whole body in comfort. She smiled.

The fisherman, searching for the most appropriate clothing he had for a woman, which was hard among his heavy-duty, rugged fishing clothes, paused, raised his gaze and stared at the vision before him. Bathed in firelight, her skin a delicate orange now, her green eyes sparkling with the firelight, her jet-black hair resting on her shoulder, silver streak melting into the tangle, this selkie woman was truly mesmerising.

'What that?' she repeated, pointing to the fire.

The fisherman snapped out of his daydream, and answered suddenly, 'Oh, it's a fire. It is very hot and keeps us warm. Do you like it?'

'Yes, I like.' The selkie woman smiled, her eyes still fixed upon the dancing flames. Everything in this strange world on land was new and exciting. She had forgotten the pull of the sea and the pain of being separated from her skin. Right there and then, with the feel of a blanket, the fire, the walls around her, the golden sunlight flowing through the window, she forgot for a moment her home beneath the waves, the cold and the dark. She forgot the towering, swaying kelp forests, and the fish, large and small. She forgot the struggle to stay alive, to fight for food and stay away from danger. This house, these stone walls with their fire and safety, was a million miles away from that world, whilst still being but a stone's throw from it. This new world was mesmerising, safe and happy. As the fisherman began to dress her with clothes for the first time, she watched as he was forever careful to avert his gaze from her body, being respectful and gentlemanly. This confused the selkie as this was not how the animalistic, passionate selkie men acted, focused only on one thing. This is the reason the selkie women lived in groups without the men. But this man, this fisherman, was kind and gentle. The selkie felt something she had not felt before and it confused her greatly, but she enjoyed this feeling very much.

Time passed, as time has a tendency of doing. Each day the fisherman left to farm the seas and, as he told the selkie, to look for her skin. Each night the fisherman returned, nets full of fish but no seal skin to be found. Of course, he knew where it was all along. He had moved it since that moonlit night many weeks ago. It now lay safe, under the rocks that made up the wall that protected the limpet cottage on the cliff, safe and hidden for all time. At first, the selkie had a heavy heart each day with no seal skin, but this pain and upset eased over the weeks, as pain is known to do, until the missing skin became just a dull ache, like that of a now-healed injury, occasionally flaring up when rain is on the way. There were nights, when the moon was bright and the sea was calm, and the sound of the pipes came drifting over the breeze, when the selkie felt heavy-hearted. She began to seek comfort in the strong, safe arms of the fisherman, laying with him by the fire, basking in his and the fire's warmth. The closeness of their bodies, her soft, smooth skin against his tough, leathery hide, caused sparks, the like of which neither of them had felt before. Then, one full moon, as the fire blazed and the waves pounded the rocks below, a warm fireside embrace went further. Their lips met. Hands began exploring each other's bodies. Limbs became entwined. Mind, body and soul became one.

Over the next year or so, the selkie became part of the human world. She took a human name, Muriel, meaning 'The Shining Sea'. The fisherman thought this fitting, as her eyes, as dark green as they were, sparkled still in the faintest of light, as waves do when catching the last of the evening sun. Muriel took on the jobs the fisherman struggled to do. She would go to market to sell the catch each day. She swiftly found that a smile and a 'Hullo, hoo are you?' would set up the bargaining well with the traders, who always lit up when they saw her coming. She was allowed to keep some of the money for herself by the fisherman, for she managed to get an even greater price for the fish than he ever could. Her soft, female charms and the ocean-deep eyes made the men putty in her hands. This gave her power, which she enjoyed, but never felt the need to abuse. She was comfortable and safe in this new world. The money she saved, and bought herself new clothes: long, practical, warm dresses, that hugged her top but billowed and flowed in the wind from her waist to her ankles, many layers giving movement and shape to her wandering. They were no seal skin, but they were good enough for now.

In time, her clothes became tight around her belly. Her stomach swelled and the fisherman realised she was with child. Excited by the prospect of having a wee bairn on the way, but worried what would be said if the child was born out of wedlock, on one wet, rough day, when the fishing had to wait, he escorted Muriel to the local church where the parson joined them in matrimony. Muriel had no real idea of what this meant. The fisherman tried to explain, tried to tell her this meant they would be together, forever, linked through this sacred bond, but Muriel was confused. How could a ring on a finger and some words bind you any more than the child they shared now growing in her belly?

The waves smashed violently against the rocks, rain hitting sideways onto the pocket of warmth in which the fisherman held the selkie's hand as beads of sweat ran from her head. Her brow wrinkled. She raised her head and screamed. The baby was coming, whether they were ready or not. The fisherman had not had time to go and get help. It had happened in the dead of night, all too quickly, and now, the infant was on its way. With a crash of thunder and a flash of lightning, into the world came Guthrie, meaning 'Windy Place', which their home certainly was that night. His eyes were as dark green and bottomless as his mother's, his skin pale and white, his head covered in thick, dark hair.

Being first-time parents, living outside of a community on the border of the land and sea, brings many issues and worries. The fisherman was used to sleepless nights, long days at sea, and being busy, but being a father hit him hard. If Guthrie had a restless night, it meant the fisherman and Muriel had little to no sleep. But the fish would not catch themselves and, without fish to sell, there would be no coin to buy food and clothing for the baby. The fisherman found himself out at sea, eyelids wanting to close, hands slipping from the oars, fish slipping from the nets. Despite this, the fisherman and the selkie were strong together and they watched as Guthrie grew. When he began to crawl, the knives and sharp instruments used to fix and mend the fishing equipment went up high. When walking began, blankets and cushions covered the harsh edges of the stone hearth and tiled floor. Then, as life seemed to become manageable, and the couple had settled into parenthood, learning how to delight and find joy in the smallest of things, from a laugh to a new skill Guthrie had learnt, Muriel's belly began to grow once more.

Their second child came quicker than the first, as it happens most of the time. On a sunny afternoon, when the ocean was flat calm and the sun streamed into the tiny cottage windows, this time with a local midwife in situ, baby number two was born. A little girl this time, blessed the family. Eilidh was the name that came to their lips. Eilidh, radiant one, radiant like the sun that blazed in the sky when she was born.

The couple soon found that the second child, with her dark hair and dark green eyes, was easier than the first. Like the muscle memory of hauling in the nets, the fisherman and Muriel slipped back into the old routines of restless nights, but had learnt to revel in the smallest of pleasures Eilidh brought them, and their hearts melted when Eilidh's big brother, now a toddler fast growing into a child, was smitten by his sister. They became inseparable.

Life became easier and easier as the children grew, became more independent and started to help out around the house. Guthrie showed he had nimble fingers for mending the nets, and strong arms for hauling them in. He had the natural ability of reading the sea, the tides and the currents. He was happiest when on his father's boat, the waves rolling beneath him. He often trailed his fingers in the cold water of the North Sea, giving him a connection to his mother's kin. He did not know he was the son of a selkie. His parents had chosen not to tell him. But his mother had told him many, many stories as a child; stories of the sea, of the evil finn folk, the enchanting merfolk, and the elusive selkies, never once telling of her past life. Both Guthrie and Eilidh lost themselves in the stories, the detailed descriptions of the worlds beneath the waves, and the adventures of those that inhabited them. These stories connected with both children, giving them a love of the sea, as strong as that of both their parents.

Eilidh took after her mother. She was soft of hand and tongue. The home was kept spotless by her and her mother, and at market, she used her innocence and cuteness to sell even more fish and for a greater price than her mother! She, too, had a longing for the sea, though. She would push her father to take her on the boat with her brother. The fisherman refused; the sea was no place for a girl. Women were bad luck at sea, and he didn't want to bring that upon his family. So, in secret, Eilidh would slip down the cliff, slip off her clothes, and bathe in the cool waters, feeling the waves ripple and roll around her body, chill her skin, and calm her soul.

Life was fair and fine in those years, and the children grew into young adults, standing tall and beautiful beside their parents. But, despite the fishing being good, the price of fish being high, and the living being easy, Muriel became more and more troubled. Without the distraction of two young children to look after and the housework halved thanks to Eilidh's help, her thoughts often turned to the sea and to her home. She began to long for the depths of the ocean, the pressure of the icy cold water on her seal skin, the tickle of the seaweed as she weaved through the great kelp forests. She missed her life before the fisherman had stolen her skin. Yes, she loved him, of course she loved him, but he had done an unspeakable evil in her eyes. Muriel had long since realised what had happened. She had searched those rocks and swam deep into the sea around the coast many times in the days after her seal skin went missing, but had had no luck. There was no other explanation. The fisherman had taken it. She was mad, of course she was, but she was also falling in love, and the heady mix of emotions confused her mind for many weeks and months. When she became pregnant, the matter of her missing skin seemed to become trivial. She now had a young life to devote herself to. But now her children could fend for themselves, those thoughts of anger began to resurface. The little things her husband did that would grate on her began to dig deeper and deeper into her nerves. He would never put his boots away, choosing to simply kick them off at the door, leaving her to do it. He would slump in the chair and fall asleep, snoring like a winter's storm just as dinner was ready. These and many more things led to intrusive thoughts. Maybe a pillow over the face as he slept, a swift nudge in the back when they were on the cliffs, a slip of something into his broth. None of this happened as, after all was said, Muriel loved this complicated, flawed, handsome, complex man. This, though, led to her questioning her entire life with him. Was it a lie? Had she ever really loved him? Did she still love him? He had given her a home she loved and children who had become her world, and she loved him for that, but he had taken away her old life, her very being, her identity. Could they move on from this? And the fisherman, he just continued with his life, totally oblivious of the feelings and thoughts in his wife's head, the whirlwind of emotions swirling inside her, the anger, the rage, the love, and the compassion. A storm was brewing, like the early ripples on the sea and the wisps of clouds in the sky showing a change in the weather, the signs were there. A storm was brewing.

Summer was waning, August was coming to a close, and the sun was hazy in the sky. The promise of autumn was in the air. The leaves of the trees that dared to grow near the shoreline began to show the faintest tint of brown on their leaves, the horse chestnut being the first. The blackberries were fat and fast disappearing as the birds gorged themselves, readying for a lean winter. The apples were being gathered and stored in paper in barns to last the winter by the local folk, and Guthrie and Eilidh were sat on the low wall that had surrounded their cottage since before they could remember. They looked longingly out to sea and spoke of the stories their mother told them. They questioned whether they were real or not. The details their mother went into, the way she described the world beneath the waves, was as if she had beheld them with her own eyes. She spoke of these places with genuine love and longing. But these were stories, just stories passed from teller to listener for many years, nothing more. The conversation then began to shift to life for the young pair, and, being the older brother, Guthrie began to tease his little sister, suggesting she had taken a fancy to a local boy in the village. The twinkle in her eye when the lad's name was mentioned by her brother suggested she had, but she did not want her brother to know, so she shoved him in the shoulder. Guthrie wobbled, lost his balance and began to fall, almost in slow motion, backwards, off the wall, into the yard. His hand grasped the coping stone he was sat upon, which caused it to shift and move before his fall was broken by the flagstones of the cottage yard. He wasn't hurt, but worried he had broken the wall. He stood up swiftly and he and Eilidh saw, where the coping stone had sat and was now dislodged, there was a hollow between the inner and outer stones of the wall. They noticed this space was not empty, as expected, but was filled with a parcel wrapped in brown, waxed paper, tied in brown string. Their father was out at sea and their mother was running errands in the village. Alone, they stood there looking at this package, wondering what it might be and how long it had been there. The cobwebs suggested it was older than they were. With curiosity taking hold and getting the best of them, they both pulled the package out of the void in the wall.

With their hearts in their mouths, eyes darting this way and that to see if they were being observed, they untied the bundle, peeled back the wax paper, and saw it: the treasure concealed inside. As the sun shone down on the backs of their necks, it caught the fine, silky seal hair that was seeing the light of day for the first time in almost two decades. The children marvelled as they unfolded the creaseless, perfect seal skin. Instantly they knew what this was. This was no ordinary seal skin from a wild seal – this was their mother's. The stories she told, the way she gazed longingly upon the sea, the sorrowful songs she would sing at night when she thought they were all sleeping. It all made perfect sense now. Their mother was a selkie.

Their mother was a selkie, which meant they were half-selkies themselves! Words and half-phrases whipped between the siblings, both trying hard to comprehend what had happened. Why was this here? Who had put it there? It surely wasn't their father, was it? Could he be capable of stealing their mother's seal skin, forcing her into a life on land, and marriage to him? Could anyone be so cruel and selfish? Not their father, they thought, the kindly fisherman that would do anything for anyone if asked, who would pick them up and hold them tight if they had a fall, who showed such devotion to his wife, such love. If he had stolen this skin and hidden it, they felt as if they didn't actually know their father at all! Did their mother know he had done this? Should they tell her? Surely, she deserved to have her skin back, after all of these years, for it was a part of her, after all.

The children decided, after much debate, to wrap it up and hide it in the house. Their mother was the first back, singing a mournful tune as she walked down the cliff path to the house as she came. The children noticed the sadness in her voice, the melancholy tones that could pluck the leaves from the trees and take the joy and majesty from a sunset. But then came the low baritone voice of the fisherman, singing a shanty as he crunched his boat to shore and stepped on land, unloading his catch. Now was not the time, the children thought. They would have to wait if they wanted to return to their mother what was rightfully hers.

The time came a few weeks later. The tide was perfect and saw the fisherman up early to make the most of the calm and catch a boat full of fish. He tried his hardest to drag his son out of his bed to come and enjoy the day's fishing with him, as there was no use staying home watching his mother mend nets. Guthrie put on a gravelly voice and faked an illness, rolling over and going back to sleep. Once the fisherman's boat was nothing more than a speck on the horizon, Eilidh and Guthrie gathered their mother into the house. They sat her by the fire and Eilidh produced, from under her bed, a wrap of brown paper.

'This is yours, mother, we are certain of it. We know not why or when this happened, but we know it must be yours…' started Eilidh, before being cut off by her brother.

'The stories you told us, of the world beneath the waves… they're true, aren't they? We know they are. Only someone who has seen those wonders first-hand can describe them the way you have. This must be yours.'

The siblings watched as their mother's fingers untied the course brown string that bound the parcel and folded back the brown paper. They watched as their mothers' eyes filled with salty tears and her fingers ran through the soft seal fur of the skin on her lap. They watched, then they held her, tightly, in a warm embrace. The three of them said not a word, their shoulders occasionally shuddering upwards as they cried tears of joy and sadness.

After what seemed like an age and no time at all, the trio left their embrace and looked at each other. The children explained to their mother what they had done, how they found the skin in the wall, and how they had wondered what had happened. Then, with a large intake of breath, Muriel, beholding her beautiful children, told her story. She had told them many stories, there, in front of the fire, in that little cottage on the cliffs. But this time… this time it was so much more than a story. For this time, it was the truth. She told of her home under the sea, and the wonders there. She told of the ritual dancing under the full moon and of that fateful night she thought she had lost her skin. The children listened in total silence. She told of their father and the kindness he had shown her when she lost her skin. No, wait. She had not lost it. He had taken it! The children saw rage shoot across their mother's face as she let her emotions flood out of her. He had taken her skin on purpose. He had forced her to stay on land. He had been the reason she had not returned home for these many years. Home, beneath the waves, the cold water, the towering kelp forests, the fish of all shapes and sizes. Home. And with this thought, the anger washed away, and a smile crept onto Muriel's face. Her hands raised her seal skin to her cheek and, as a toddler would snuggle their special blanket, she nestled her face in her special skin. She stared, stared beyond the fire and into her own memories. The thought of being able to go back filled her heart with glee.

'You want to go back, don't you?' asked Eilidh, who had always been the most empathetic of the two children. 'But what about us? We will miss you. Will you return?'

Their mother snapped back to the cottage, and she looked at them. Her husband, the fisherman... what he had done, stealing her skin away, was unforgivable, no matter how much she had grown to love him. And she did love him, truly she did. But he had given her two things, more precious than all the gems in the world. Before her now sat her children. Without the fisherman and his most unforgivable action, she would not have been blessed with her children, whom she loved beyond all things. Did this justify the fisherman's actions? Muriel's heart was divided, her head split in two. Out of such evil came such beauty and good. What was she to do? She had meant to slip into her seal skin and return to the waves, never looking back, never explaining to the fisherman what had happened, leaving him to forever wonder what had happened. But that would mean leaving her children. She could not do that; her heart would break.

Guthrie spoke, 'But mother, if you are a selkie, what does that make us? We have no seal skins, but we are your children. We both share a connection with the sea.'

Again, a smile brought Muriel back from thought, as a ray of hope dawned.

'Of course, my gorgeous children, of course! Guthrie, you are so clever, I forget how clever you are sometimes and that is my mistake.' Muriel addressed the children, full of love and hope. 'You are my children as much as you are your father's, which means you can come to the sea with me! But not just yet. There will be a night – or so the stories tell, the stories of those rare selkie folk who settle with people from the land – a night when the moon is full, sometime around your eighteenth birthday. On that night you will know, and you will hear. You will hear the music as we come to land and dance under the pale moonlight, and you will know it is your time. Come to us then, and we will clothe you in your new skin and you can come to the water with us, if this is what you want.'

'Oh yes, mother, yes! More than anything, this is what I want,' replied Eilidh, having always been closest to her mother.

'I, erm, I…' Guthrie, having spent much of his life with his father since he could make himself useful on the boat, was unsure about leaving him. 'Can I return to live on land from time to time?'

'This is a choice, a hard one, which you must make,' answered his mother, her voice full of love and care. 'For once you don your seal skin, you are committing to a life under the sea, allowed only to come to shore on a full moon to dance, play, and sing. But you do not have to make your mind up just yet.'

Muriel lost herself once more in the fire, watching the flames flicker and dance. 'I shall leave tonight, before your father returns. The fishing is good today, he will be gone until the morning, and when he arrives, I will be gone.'

The children were shocked at the suddenness of their mother's actions. They asked if it had to be so soon, but Muriel could not bear to look into those eyes – the eyes of her husband who had lied to her for so many years; the eyes that had hidden the truth from her, robbed her of her life; the eyes that had been so kind and loving, yet hidden such treachery. Her heart and mind were set. Now she knew her children could follow her when they had come of age, she knew tonight was the night, no later.

The sun set with a glorious burst of fire in the sky and the mellow evening engulfed the shore. A low sea mist rolled in, looking like a thin blanket over the sea. The children and their mother stood by the lapping waves of the cold sea. They watched their mother slip off her dress, exposing her ivory skin to the waxing crescent moon. It was a night that held no magic, but yet was full of wonder, as the children watched their life, the woman that bore them, gave them life, raised them and loved them, cared for them when they were ill or hurt, held them when they were sad, slip on the silky, furry seal skin and transform into a large-eyed seal, lying on the rocks. The seal blinked slowly before hauling its bulk awkwardly around and slipping into the depths with barely a ripple. And with that, no fanfare, Muriel the selkie, the mother, the captive, the wife, was gone, returned to her old life.

And so ends her story, but not this story, for there are still three players left in this game of life that we all must play. A game of truth, dare, and lies. Soon enough, one of the players was to face the consequences of their actions.

The sun was rising in a misty sky. Autum's calling card was in the air, for she was waiting her turn to come into the world. A speck appeared on the horizon, getting closer and closer. The fisherman landed his boat and excitedly hauled his catch up the sloped path to the cottage.

'Muriel!' he shouted, his voice full of excitement and pride. 'Wife! Love of my life! Come and see the catch I have brought ashore!' His face beamed with pride as his ears strained to her his beloved's voice respond, but no voice answered his call. 'Guthrie! Eilidh! Are you there?' His voice now twinged with desperation, desperate to share his achievement with someone he loved.

The fisherman burst through the door of his cottage to find his children dragging themselves, bleary eyed, out of bed. 'Where is your mother?' he asked them.

The children looked at each other, then at their father, the man they had loved unquestioningly until the events of the day before. Their father looked upon them like a dog seeing his owner pick up the lead and put on their shoes.

It was the sweet Eilidh that spoke first. Despite the hatred that now bubbled inside of her for her father, he was still her father, and there was still a love within her heart for this flawed man. She took his hand and guided him to a seat by the embers of the fire. The man's face dropped, knowing this was not the actions of someone with good news.

'No,' he cried, 'no, she's not… tell me she's not… but she was in the best of health when I left. Was it an accident? What happened? Tell me now child!' His voice ran the gamut of emotions a mind goes through when they are faced with the possibility of the loss of a loved one. Shock, surprise, sadness, desperation, and anger, all mixed together with many more emotions besides.

Eilidh spoke softly, in the same voice her mother had used many times to calm her husband down after a bad day at sea, or to soothe the anger of her children over the frustrations of being young. 'Father, we found it.'

Instantly, the fisherman's face dropped. He knew what she meant. The look in his beautiful baby girl's face told him all he needed to know.

'And you gave it back to her, didn't you? DIDN'T YOU?' The shock gave way to rage. 'You found your mother's seal skin and gave it to her, and now she's left me, left *us*! She's gone back to the sea with nary a thought for those of us she has left behind! She's so selfish!'

And with that he caught himself, and he caught the look of bewilderment, confusion and shock in his children's faces.

'She's selfish, is she, Father?' Guthrie burst out, spitting venom towards his father. 'She's so selfish, yes, of course she is! Accepting her fate, staying on land all these years, marrying you out of pity, bearing you the children you so desperately wanted. Cooking, cleaning, selling your fish for better prices than you ever could. She gave her entire life to you, and for what?' There was fire in his eyes. Guthrie's fists were clenched by his side as he towered now over his old man. 'All that to finally find that she had been betrayed from day one! That her life on the land was a sham. That the man she thought she loved was the reason she could never go back home, to her family, to the people and places she loved!' And then Guthrie saw it. He saw the lines on his father's face. He saw the grey hairs dotted across his head and face. He saw the many summers and the equal winters in his eyes. Old man, that was true, he was now an old man. Guthrie could see this old man was now full of regret and remorse. A single tear fell from his right eye and found a crease on his leathery face to follow down to his beard line before getting lost in the salt and pepper whiskers. Guthrie too changed his temper when he saw this. He saw a man full of love for his wife, and utter regret for his selfish, knee-jerk reactions a lifetime ago.

'I didn't mean to cause her upset! Honestly, I didn't!' The fisherman began his defence of his actions, his body shaking, the tears coming faster now. 'When I saw her that night, naked, young and lithe, dancing and moving like nothing I had ever seen before, I… I… I…

'I was alone and had been for many years. I fell instantly in love with her. I knew there could never be anyone else for me. I didn't think…'

He was cut short by Guthrie and his rising anger.

'No, you didn't think, Father, and that's the problem.'

A gentle hand of his sister fell upon his arm, holding him back and calming him.

'Let him speak,' said Eilidh.

'Thank you, kind daughter,' the fisherman said to Eilidh.

'Don't thank me, Father. Thank our mother, for she was the one that taught us kindness and humility. But that will only last so long, so speak now and be quick about it.' The words came with force from Eilidh's lips, and so the fisherman pressed on.

'I took a guess at which seal skin was hers,' continued the fisherman, gazing somewhere in the middle distance. He was, in his mind, back in time, on that night when the moon shone bright and the selkies danced. 'I had heard the stories of the people from the sea from my mother, and so knew the power of the skins and what taking one would do. It wasn't hard to work out which was your mother's. It was by far the most beautiful one there, as she was. It was then simply a case of slipping it away and hiding it. Well, you know where I hid it, seeing as you found it.'

Guthrie and Eilidh stared daggers at their father.

'Well, yes, anyway,' continued the fisherman, 'the rest you can probably guess. I "helped" her look for her skin, and, of course, no skin was found. She then began to live with me and, as I hoped, one thing led to another and we... well... fell in love.'

'Was it love, though?' asked Guthrie. 'Or was it coercion? Was it control? Did she even have a choice?'

'No, it wasn't like that!' the fisherman defended his actions fervently. 'She loved me! I loved her! It wasn't about control! It wasn't! There honestly wasn't a day that went by when I didn't regret my actions; when I didn't hate myself for what I did.'

'Then why didn't you give her skin back, Father?' Eilidh's voice fell soft upon her father's ears. Despite this softness, the question cut through his mind like a knife and demanded an answer.

'I tried; I really did. Many a night I lay awake next to her, thinking I should give it back to her, but I was afraid she'd leave me. Then you and your brother came along and… and…' he hesitated, looking at them with their beautiful dark green eyes, the same eyes as their mother, '… and, I thought if I did, she would leave and take you. And, above all things, I could not live without you. You are my everything, a part of me; the best part of me.' He had now broken down completely. His head was in his hands, the emotion seeping from his eyes, his shoulders shaking with sadness, remorse and regret. 'And now I've lost her! The way she spoke of her home, in the stories she told you… it was clear if she had the chance to go back, she would never return here. She's gone forever, and it is my fate to live with the decision I made all those years ago – a decision that brought me the true love of my life, brought me you, but has led to me losing her.'

'And losing us!' Guthrie remarked. Although he could see his father was sorry for his actions, in his eyes this did not make things right. 'The first chance I get I will be leaving to join her.' And with that he turned and left, slamming the door behind him.

The fisherman continued to sob, louder now, into his hands, His life was in pieces. 'Am I to lose you, too?' he asked his daughter.

Eilidh hesitated and then answered with much control in her voice. 'Yes, you will. You will lose me, but not as soon as you will lose Guthrie. We will be able to join our mother on the next full moon after our eighteenth birthday.'

After that, Guthrie avoided his father as best he could for another year or so until he turned eighteen, and, on the next full moon, he slipped away that night without even a goodbye to his sister, knowing she would join him soon. A few years later it was Eilidh's turn. She, however, embraced her father. She still loved this flawed man. He was her father and gave her life, after all.

'Look for me on the full moon and at high tide,' she said, 'and look for me when you are at sea, for I will watch over you and your boat. You are a good man who did a bad thing for the right reason, for love, and had to live with the consequences. I can see how it has eaten you up inside. That decision brought so much happiness, and now has brought so much sadness. I love you, Father, and so does Guthrie, although he could not bring himself to say it before he left. Take care, Father.' And, with a peck on the cheek, she was gone.

From that day, when the fisherman was out at sea and the ocean was flat and calm, and the sun shone on his neck, and the fish seemed to jump into his boat, he would often spy two large, dark eyes peering from the sea's surface, watching over him. He knew this was Eilidh, bringing the calm weather and the good fortune, watching over her father. But, when the waves were high, and the storm raged, and the rain came as hard upwards from the sea as it did from the sky, the fisherman often saw the two dark eyes of Guthrie, his anger and vengeance still aimed at his father. But never was the storm so bad as to capsize him and send him to the locker, and despite the raging storm, his nets were always full of fine and fair fish. He was the only fisherman on those nights that landed any fish and could charge a fine price for them. This was Guthrie's way of showing his father he hadn't forgiven him, but he still loved him all the same.

And of Muriel, well, the fisherman never saw that beauty again. Not until one night, many years later, when the sea was calm and the moon was bright and full. The fisherman's bones creaked, his muscles ached, his hair and whiskers were as grey as the morning. He was too old for this now, but he had no choice. It was as he was hauling in his boat to moor it up that Muriel came to him. She stayed far off, just two dark eyes watching him, but he knew those eyes so well. He had gazed into them many times before and they had always brought him peace and warmth. This time was no different. He turned when the eyes disappeared beneath the surface, and dragged his carcass up the well-worn steps to his home. He left the catch and the nets for the morning, for now it was time for sleep. He fell into that bed of his, the one he had shared with his wife, and he closed his eyes for the last time: a man still full of love for his family, and regret for the moment of madness all those long years ago.

THE GHOST IN THE CAR PARK

I will start with a trigger warning for this story. One of the reasons I was keen for this book to be aimed at adults is so I could really explore the darker parts of folk tales. The story you are about to read is not, in any way, based on facts, and is totally fictitious as far as I'm aware. However, the sensitive subjects it addresses were very real for far too many women, well into the twentieth century, and these controlling behaviours are still found in modern-day society, although they are no longer accepted, and even criminalised. The story touches on rape and coercive control within a marriage, so if you feel this is a subject you'd prefer not to read about, I would advise you to skip. It is, however, a subject we should not shy away from, and we should give people the choice to engage with it or not. The highlighting of this kind of behaviour and its unacceptable nature in modern society is, I believe, the key to stamping it out.

I heard the story some years ago online. A lot of really good tellings of folk tales have been recorded and can be found amongst the tangled strands of the World Wide Web, if you know where to look. The story, like all the stories within this book, hit a chord for me, and I could relate to the modern-day main character. At the time, I was working as a part-time bar manager in my local pub, which had a window that overlooked the car park in the corridor to the toilets. We were having some troubles with a new regular who would flash the cash, but would upset the locals. The landlady was stuck between a rock and a hard place, not wanting to give up his money by barring him, but trying to keep the locals onside. In this story, the problem is solved for them, unlike real life.

I have never heard this story anywhere else, nor have I managed to track down its origins, but it holds all the hallmarks of a classic ghost story. I have used my own experiences (for the later part of the story, not the former) to bring it to life. I have also aimed to write the first half as a pastiche of a nineteenth-century Gothic horror genre, in the vein of Dracula, The Strange Case of Dr Jekyll and Mr Hyde, *and others, with the overlong, overly descriptive sentences that build the world and its characters, giving it a rich sense of time and place. It got a pass from my wife, who is a secondary school English teacher who has taught nineteenth-century Gothic horror many times, so, here it is. Just remember, this is only a story. No need to have nightmares...*

It was a house like all the others that rose from the cobbled road that meandered toward the centre of town. Standing three storeys high, it shared its walls with its neighbours, along with its early Georgian style. The houses themselves were but two decades old when this tale began, and were seen by many as a statement from those who owned and lived in them to those that would look on in envy at their wealth and standing within the community. This was a view very much taken by the house's current occupant and owner. The man now living in this opulence and elegance was a one Mr Pemberton. He had risen from his working-class background by means of the opportunities afforded to him through his connections made within the coal mines, such as the now late Mr Wilkes, who had owned a great many of the pits. Keen of mind and quick-thinking, Pemberton used his intimidating size to broker deals with all the right people, ensuring his pockets were well-lined. Starting his life in the mines, he grew tall and strong, but longed for more time in the daylight. Now he had garnered the favour of several wealthy backers, he had become the owner of several local mining establishments, many of them gifted to him by Wilkes for lack of a male heir on his part, employing many hundreds of men in his service.

Pemberton worked hard but, equally, enjoyed his nights in the local tavern. He was, after all, from working stock, and his fancy for ale never left him, nor did his fancy for the finer gender. He was well known to have a different woman on his knee every night, whether that woman wanted to be there or not. He had met his wife when she was but 15 years of age, a young slip of a lass, fair of hair, slim of waist, and a natural beauty. She was the daughter of one of the supervisors at Pemberton's most productive mine. He had set his eyes on this beauty early on, so when she turned 16, Pemberton ensured her father's consent to marry by guaranteeing his job for the next few years, and that their house would stay standing. The girl was now his and, during the day, she brought life to an otherwise soulless house. There were several servants in the employment of Mr Pemberton. There was the butler: an older gentleman who had, like his master, come from a working-class background and made a name for himself in the service trade (hence being headhunted by Pemberton). Below the butler were the housemaid and the scullery maid, both in their early twenties and fair to look at. Most importantly for Pemberton, they kept their mouths shut. They did not partake in idle chitter-chatter, preferring to ensure the work was done to the high, exacting standard their master put upon them. Pemberton was known for coming down hard on his female servants if they had not met the required benchmarks with their duties.

Young Mrs Pemberton's life was carefree for the most part, or so it would seem to those looking in from the outside. The staff attended to her every whim, and she wanted for nothing. She kept her head low, and her mouth closed, just the way Pemberton liked it – for she had seen how he treated the young servant maids when they had stepped out of line, and she worried she too would meet a similar fate. She asked no questions when he was back late in the evenings, and would simply lie there letting her man fulfil his cardinal desires. However, there was no desire on her part. Every night her eyes may have been closed, but her ears were on high alert, waiting to hear the front door open, before her inebriated husband stumbled his bulk up the finely carpeted staircase toward the marital chambers.

Upon the night when our story begins, Mrs Pemberton was lying in bed, listening to the grandfather clock tick and chime the hours away. The servants had long since gone to bed and the house was now silent and dark. She had extinguished the candle by her bedside and now lay staring into the pitch dark above the bed. The chamber drapes were of a heavy material that let no light through, even on a bright summer's day, and could catch and muffle sounds, stopping them from escaping the room. Not a single glimmer of light from the street made its way into the void of her room. She listened as the clock struck twelve, but, to her surprise, there was no opening of the front door. She listened once more until the clock struck the quarter hour and still no sign of her inebriated husband. Her mind began to race as to why this could be. Naturally, being not ignorant to her husband's true nature, her thoughts turned to him with another woman. Mrs Pemberton cared not if this was the case, for this would mean he would leave her alone that night and she may sleep easier. As her husband was getting older, though, now in his fifties, he did this less and less. The women had found ways to avoid his grabbing hands, and had the measure of him. Where once he had been the envy of every man, now he was becoming the butt of their jokes behind his back. Although they were not outright directed at him, Pemberton knew how the others within the tavern mocked him in hushed tones. Anger swelled inside him, alongside a longing to regain the vigour and prowess of his youth. With these feelings bubbling beneath the surface, he would stumble home and take it out on his wife. She would still be willing to please her husband and to do her wifely duty. But this night something had happened.

Word was circulating within the groups of men in the tavern, of the conversations their wives had during the day while the men were at work. It seemed certain allegations had been made of the hulking pit owner – allegations from within his own household. This, Pemberton knew, could not be allowed to take root. This seed of dissent and discord needed to be removed before it germinated into stronger accusation and investigation. Pemberton followed a gentlemen from a nearby table, whom he had overheard discussing the gossip from his household, to the toilets. The gentleman was dressed in a green jacket and bowler, such was the fashion, and sporting a fine pair of mutton chops either side of his face. There, before the gentleman had time to begin his ablutions, Pemberton took the man firmly by the back of his neck with one hand and held securely the gentleman's right hand with the other. Holding him tight, Pemberton firmly insisted the gentleman told him of the conversation he had been having before coming to relieve himself, of who else knew of this, and of where this scandalous nonsense originated. The gentleman, feeling the strength in Pemberton's hands – strength gained from his days underground working the coalface – feared for his safety and thought this news was not secret enough to risk his life over. Besides, it was about Pemberton anyway, and this would give him a chance to get his house in order, thought the gentleman.

After receiving the full story from the bowler-hatted gentleman in the tavern conveniences, Pemberton returned to the bar, where he ordered another pint of ale and a whisky chaser. The green-jacketed gentleman slipped away out the back door so as not to be seen, as requested by Pemberton. His bloody nose and swollen eye would have been hard to explain away to others in the tavern, thought Pemberton. He sat drinking his pint slowly and thoughtfully, considering carefully what he was to do about the situation and how this would be put right. A man in his position could not be seen like this, for it is simply not good for business. By the time his glass was drained and the whisky had been knocked back in a single swig, the alcohol had hit him with full force. He normally drank a lot each night; however, this was more than even he would normally drink, and the room was now spinning. Staggering, although trying hard to steady himself to save face, he proceeded out the tavern as the barman followed, bolting the door. Closing time had long gone, but nobody, not even the landlord, dared tell Pemberton to drink up and leave – especially in his current state of mind and inebriation.

The clock had not long since struck a single chime in the darkness when the young Mrs Pemberton heard keys at the door, like a carriage rattling down the street. The door, after some persuading, opened with a creak and slammed too shortly thereafter. She listened to hear her husband's heavy, staggering footsteps, not heading up the stairs, but toward the back of the house for a moment – before thundering, booming step after booming step, up the stairs toward her.

This time, Mrs Pemberton knew something was different, and so she turned her head to see the door to the marital chambers slowly creak open. Her husband had managed to light the gas lamp on the landing and now stood silhouetted against the light. She saw that bulk which she knew would soon be on her. His hulking, sweaty mass pushing down upon her, shovel-like hands pulling and tearing at her nightwear. She dreaded the feeling of being violated, but this is what marriage was, she naïvely thought: pleasing her man. The pain was always there, but she never showed it. A moan and a groan through gritted teeth and, within a matter of minutes, he was done, and he would roll over and sleep with his naked body on full show. This would make Mrs Pemberton shudder with disgust. She would also sob and cry for an hour or so the first few years of the marriage, as this was not how she dreamt of wedded bliss. But now, she would steel herself against the upset and the anger.

But tonight? Tonight was different.

Pemberton froze at the doorway longer than usual, considering carefully in his foggy mind what he was about to do. The alcohol and anger clouded his brain, but this seemed to him in that moment to be the best and right course of action.

In the faint gaslight, Mrs Pemberton saw that the figure of her husband looked different. He swayed more than usual, and he had something in his hand that glittered and glinted in the pale light. He stepped forward. All of a sudden, he was upon her on the bed. Once more, she noticed this was different. No clawing at her nightclothes, not even a removal of the sheets. Her husband simply straddled her, knees either side of her chest. His left hand held both her hands tightly above her head. She had learnt to keep quiet, no matter what he did. To call out would only result in some kind of physical punishment, and the cry would not get past the heavy drapes. Mr Pemberton could do what he liked to her in that bedroom and the world outside would never know – or so he had thought.

'Why did you have t' open ya big fat mouth?' The words were gravel; rough like sandpaper and full of anger and emotion. 'Ya stupid chattin' will be the end o' me, and I won't be havin' it!'

As her husband raised his right hand, she saw the glinting object for what it was, and Mrs Pemberton realised what had happened. Three days prior she had been in conversation with Mrs Waverly from two doors down. She was from a good middle-class family and took pity on the young Mrs Pemberton, all alone for so long in that large house, only the staff for company and that brutish husband of hers. She had taken Mrs Pemberton under her wing and would regularly come for tea and cake around the house. On this particular occasion, Mrs Waverly had noticed a discolouration on the young woman's neck. Mrs Waverly was not one to let things go unnoticed or un-investigated, so she began to pry into Mrs Pemberton's doings. Before long, Mrs Pemberton had opened up to Mrs Waverly (in complete confidence) about her life with her brutal husband, their loveless marriage, his violence towards her, and her nightly ordeals that she had come to accept. Mrs Waverly was not accepting any of this. She was a firm believer in the rights of women and the right to be able to say no to their husbands, for their body was their own. This got Mrs Pemberton's mind to thinking. Could she get out of this hell on Earth? Was there a way out?

Mrs Pemberton had told all this to her in the strictest of confidence, but it was clear to her now that her trust had been misplaced, and her secrets told to others. They had made their way from mouth to ear in one form or another, and now had ended up in the ears of her rageful husband.

Mrs Pemberton found herself paralysed with fear. Her body had decided not to act upon this: no fight or flight for her, just freeze, with her senses in a heightened state. So it was that in this state, Mrs Pemberton was aware of the faintest of sounds finding its way through the curtains. It was rain on the windows. For her to be able to hear it meant it must have been biblical in its nature, and it was. It came down in vertical lines, soaking the streets all around. There was a sudden flash of lightning, which found the smallest of cracks between the window drapes A sudden slit of bright light illuminated the crazed man's face – a face full of bitterness and resentment for what his young bride had done to his reputation. That briefest of flashes also splintered off the kitchen knife now drawing ever closer to her neck. Seconds later the thunder followed. Long and low it rumbled, like rocks in an avalanche tumbling down the hill. This noise was accompanied by another, higher in pitch and just as menacing to any who heard it. Which, in this case, was the individual responsible for the actions that created this sound. The scream that shot from the poor, young, helpless Mrs Pemberton's gaping mouth lasted but a second before it drowned in gurgles and coughs. She felt the cold blade ripping and tearing at her throat. The skin gave way, giving access to the muscles and tendons beneath, which in turn parted to let the murder weapon slice through arteries, the throat and the voice box. She felt the warmth of her own blood trickle down the sides of her neck, down her front and pool onto the sheets beneath. As more and more of her blood stained the bed, more and more of her life left her.

There was another flash of lightning and, in that light, she once again saw her husband's face and, in that moment, that she had her final thoughts. They were thoughts of anger at the way she had been treated by this abhorrent man, of sadness for a life wasted indoors waiting to be raped night after night, and vengeance for all that he had done to make her life a misery. By the time the thunder had caught up to its running mate, mere seconds later, the life had left the young girl's body. But a final thought remained in her brain, staring at the dark, empty world through unblinking eyes: a thought of revenge against all men who would seek to use and abuse women. She vowed, with the last moments of her consciousness, that she would not let death be the last of her. She would return, to come back to this world as a spirit of vengeance. She would be the one who stood up to these controlling men, who sought to use women for their own selfish means, whether it be to climb the social ladder, or even simpler, for basic sexual pleasure on their part alone. Those men who would care not about the feelings of women, throwing them aside when they had finished with them like an overworn pair of shoes – they were the ones Mrs Pemberton would seek out from beyond the grave.

Life for Mrs Pemberton was short and tinged with sadness toward the end, but few ever knew of this. Mr Pemberton used his connections and curried favours from many an individual in influential places to brush this unfortunate situation under the carpet. A few deals later and a pocket now a bit lighter in coins and notes, Mr Pemberton was off the hook. The police released him with no charges, the case going down as a case of hysteria on Mrs Pemberton's side and self-defence for her husband. This came as no surprise to those who had heard the rumours before that terrible night, of the unhappy wife indoors and the way she was treated. They knew that Mr Pemberton would simply buy the loyalty of those involved and pay for his freedom. This was just what was done. Those with money, power, and influence never had anything to fear. It was not about what you knew, or who you knew, but what you knew *about* who you knew that helped you get along in this world, and got you out of all kinds of scrapes, something Mr Pemberton knew all too well.

Mr Pemberton went on to live a very long and productive life, remarrying several times over the years, always women far younger than himself. These women always went missing in the most peculiar of ways, but never did anything seem to stick to the famous 'rags to riches' Mr Pemberton. Eventually, at the ripe old age of 76, Mr Pemberton cashed in his chips to chance it on the other side. He was buried in a large tomb in the local cemetery. Despite his promiscuities, he never managed to sire an heir. It seemed he was barren and could not father any children, though not for lack of trying. This meant all his hard-won fortune and estate was divided up to many distant family members, and his business assets purchased by rival collieries. In time, Mr Pemberton became nothing but a footnote in history, a blip on the radar, an insignificant line in the book of our existence.

Now, we come forward in time to continue our story, some 150 years or so. The once middle class, three-storey town house was now a public house, having been converted into one around the turn of the twentieth century. After Mr Pemberton had moved out of his residence some twelve months after that fateful stormy night and settled in a larger house on the edge of town, the property lay empty for many years. People locally knew the rumours of what had happened and thought it ill-advised to live in such a seemingly cursed house. Over the years, people's fears had come true, with many a report of strange noises being heard from within the walls of the property. In the early 1900s, an entrepreneur purchased the houses either side of the old Pemberton residence for a very good price, due to the stories of the haunting of the middle house, and took control of this one also. Now owning the three adjoined homes, he decided to convert the ground floor into a spacious and roomy pub to serve the growing population in the area due to the continued success of the coal mines, with the rooms above becoming flats and residences for local workers.

Nobody lived there for long, however, as many reported strange goings-on within the flats. Strange screams and thumping could be heard, mostly coming from the middle house, and reports of a shadowy female figure lurking in the corners of rooms were commonplace. But, puzzlingly, these stories came only from the *men* who lived there. The public house on the ground floor, however, thrived. There were many sharings of the stories of the strange happenings and the hauntings in the building, but this all added to the allure of the establishment, bringing in people from far and wide who hoped to experience the ghostly goings-on.

Sometime in the twentieth century though, things started to slow down for the public house. The current landlord was struggling to keep trade alive, and had been resisting the pressure to go the way of many pubs and convert to a gastropub. He assured his regulars that his establishment would continue to be a true drinker's pub, where the only food being served were the crisps, nuts, and snacks from behind the bar. If customers wanted a meal, they could go next door to the kebab shop – which many of them did after a long session on a Friday night.

It was when times were hardest that Patrick Murphy came into the story, known commonly as simply Murphy. Here was a large, sturdy man, self-made and proud of his background. His family had moved over from Ireland many generations ago, so Murphy was as English as the next man, yet he clung to his Irish heritage like a hungry wolf to a rare scrap of meat. Much like Mr Pemberton all those years ago, he had worked his way up through the ranks, this time as a builder, and now owned his own small building firm. His firm's reputation wasn't the greatest, with corners being cut on a regular basis and a score of unhappy customers. But, in the days before social media, Murphy didn't have a care, for he would just move on to the next victim, or 'customer', as they would normally be described. He had a large, powerful BMW sat on the drive outside his large, impressive house, but he travelled around mostly in his work van with the company logo 'MBC' (Murphy's Building Contractors) emblazoned on the side. He was proud of what he'd achieved and wanted to show the world. Murphy was married, yet you would not believe so to see how he carried himself when not at home, which was most of the time. He liked the opposite sex, a lot. A wink here, a cheeky slap on the rear there, and not to forget the ever-popular catcall to the fine young ladies passing by the building site. Murphy liked to think of himself as God's gift to women. He believed he could have any woman he liked, and never hesitated to tell anyone who would listen. The fact he was now in his forties with his hair fast racing away from his eyebrows and new wrinkles appearing by the week didn't bother him. He still *felt* like he was in his twenties, and that was all that mattered. Besides, he would always say, 'You're only as young as the girl you feel,' right before grabbing the posterior of a young twenty-something at the bar.

Murphy had begun to frequent The Miner's Drop, as the public house had been named, in homage to the majority of its patrons when it first opened its doors. Murphy liked the lager they had on tap: not too cold and easy to drink. Of course, he insisted it had nothing to do with him being barred from practically every other pub in the town. Every night he came in, around half past five in the evening, when he finished work. Murphy would sit in his favourite place at the bar, downing pint after pint, throwing his hard-earned money around, thinking his wealth could buy him friends. What Murphy had not realised in his four decades on this planet is that money doesn't make you popular. For all the wealth he'd accumulated, for all the money he'd made, his attitude aligned more with the former owner of the building than of a modern man's. For Murphy, the women's rights movement never happened, and feminists were all lesbians who burned their bras at the weekend. As the drink went down, the profanity increased. By around 9 p.m. (when Murphy was fast approaching a dozen pints) the air was a deep shade of navy with the foul language spewing from Murphy's mouth, and the regulars were leaving. They had heard enough and begun to feel uncomfortable. They did not much care for the profanities and the convoluted stories that dribbled from the lips of this drunkard, who seemed to make it his point to inform everyone in the room of his tales, whether they wanted to hear them or not.

This went on, night after night, much to the landlord's dismay. He watched on as fewer and fewer people frequented the bar, and more and more people complained about the foul-mouthed builder. He considered barring Murphy, as Murphy went against everything the landlord agreed with, and he was ruining the atmosphere of the house. With business already struggling, this thorn in his side saw it getting worse. But then the landlord saw the money the faux Irishman put behind the bar every night. With the loss of so many patrons, this cash was much needed, and the landlord was unsure if his former clientele would return when they heard of Murphy's barring, or whether they'd stay loyal to their new drinking den. This was certainly a conundrum – one that would, luckily for the landlord, soon be taken off his hands and dealt with for him.

It was a Friday night much like any other. The regulars that still braved coming into the The Miner's were drinking and sharing stories of their week at the various tables around the room. It got to 6 p.m. and people realised there was no Murphy yet. This got hopes up that maybe they would be treated to a night off – or, even better still, that he had taken his business, foul language, and tired, misogynistic stories elsewhere. By a quarter past the hour, as the customers' moods were buoyant and merry, Murphy waltzed in like a black storm cloud chasing the sun. He was all smiles and grinning from ear to ear, yet the mood as he swept in darkened around him. Heads sank all around, eyes looking into pints.

'Top of the evening to ya' all!' came the booming, joyful voice of the man nobody wanted to see. His accent was still as British as ever before, but Murphy never let a little thing like that get in the way of cultural heritage or his happy mood.

Arriving at the bar, he slapped a crisp £20 note on the wood and whistled for the barman. The barman was serving someone else, and had others who were waiting, but he knew you didn't keep Murphy waiting. It just was not worth the aggravation. He finished up serving his customer before heading down the bar to serve the VIP his usual. The customer who had expected to be next glared at Murphy and tried to complain to the barman. But he was shot down in flames by Murphy, who arrogantly stated his importance to the pub, and said it was *his* money that kept this place open, and if the customers did not like it then they could go elsewhere – which this customer promptly did. This sharp exit by yet another valued regular caused the barman to shoot a look of desperation and disbelief at the landlord, who was perched at the other end of the bar. The landlord knew what the barman was implying; they had had this conversation almost nightly after the doors had closed. The barman could see how toxic Murphy was and the damage he was doing to the public house, and he worried about his job and the happiness of the locals, who had also complained at length to him. But the landlord just shrugged. What could he do?

Murphy explained, over the course of the next few hours, how he had had a great week. His lads finished a job a week ahead of schedule, yet they got the customer to pay even more than they had quoted as they had done extras for them. Murphy, not caring of his reputation at this point, explained how they had not really done the extras and had cut corners – just enough to get the building inspector to sign it off, but enough to increase the profit on the job so he could afford a new car. Of course, the regulars did not engage with any of this, silently wishing he would just drink up and go.

By 10 p.m., having celebrated his latest victory over the gullible Joe Public and deciding to have a chaser with every pint, trying hard to get through the entire top shelf of liquor, Murphy staggered off to the toilets – announcing this to everyone and that he would be back, and that nobody should take his seat or there would be trouble.

The room breathed a sigh of relief at this briefest of respites. Due to the layout of the public house and the modern extensions on the back, the toilets were located off a corridor, in which was a window that overlooked the rear of the properties, now used as a customer car park. After relieving himself, mostly in the urinal, Murphy staggered out and up the corridor. He stopped suddenly. Outside, the sky was dark as pitch with no moon or stars, as they were covered by heavy storm clouds. A few spots of rain had found the window, but Murphy could see clearly out into the car park, which was lit by a single floodlight on the back of the property, above the aperture he stood in front of. There in the car park he saw her. His eyes fell on a young woman. She wore a flowing white dress, and had fair hair that flowed over her shoulders, and a figure that was sleek and slim. Murphy, despite the amount of alcohol in his system, felt instantly aroused. As he looked on, mouth open wide, his hand thoughtlessly drifting towards where it had been moments before (but this time for a wholly different reason), the young woman reached out a slender arm and, with delicate fingers, beckoned him out. Murphy's heart raced. He was never one to turn down a woman's advances. But, he thought to himself, he still had half a pint left, and he had to let everyone know he was about to get lucky. He put up a finger to the woman, then pointed to the bar, made the universal sign for drink, then gestured that he would return before finishing with a few hip thrusts, just so the woman knew what he had in mind, if it wasn't already obvious. He thought to himself that he had still got it!

Bursting into the bar, Murphy slumped onto his stool, downed his pint and proudly declared what had happened to him and he was about to get lucky – but with many more profanities, curses, and lewd movements to illustrate what he was going to do to this lucky young lady. The people in the bar watched and listened in stunned silence, not because of the language used and the movements, but because they had all heard the stories of the ghost in the car park. They had heard the old tales and rumours about what had happened in this place many years ago; of the hauntings, and the strange goings-on. The lady in the car park had been seen many times before, but nobody had gone to her. Nobody could ever be that stupid, they thought. Now, however, they were being proved wrong, Murphy was just the type of person who could be that stupid.

Fuelled by alcohol, lust, and a lack of any morality to speak of, Murphy was about to go and try his luck with a vengeful spirit – so it seemed. The regulars were stunned and faced a moral conundrum. Did they tell Murphy what they knew about this woman, of her being but a ghost... or did they let their curiosity win and leave him to go to her, whilst watching to see what happened? As it was, they did not have much time to contemplate this before he was off back out the bar towards the toilets.

Murphy used the emergency exit to burst out into the car park after that young woman, who was still there, waiting for him. The customers all just sat, paralysed for a while in shock, not knowing what to do. All of a sudden, they were roused from their paralysed state by a high-pitched scream emanating from the car park. For the briefest of moments, they looked at each other, before bolting en masse towards the toilet corridor, following the barman, who led the way.

When they all arrived in the corridor and looked out the window, the scene in front of them was one that haunted their dreams for many years to come. The rain had arrived, as promised by the heavy, black clouds, and was now falling like stair rods in the sky, hitting the ground hard. Flashes of lightning illuminated the scene still further, followed by the ominous rumbles of thunder, much as it had been on that fateful night all those many years ago. The onlookers beheld the body of Murphy, lying motionless upon the asphalt of the car park, his face frozen in terror and anguish. His clothes were soaked through with rain as he lay in a pool of bright white light so dazzling it hurt the observers' eyes. The light emanated from the neck of the man, flowing like water. This, however, was not the strangest of effects within the twisted diorama in front of them.

Hovering mere feet above the lifeless man on the floor was the spirit of a woman. She was what the regulars expected to have seen, but now they had beheld her in all her otherworldly glory, their hearts skipped a beat and their knees began to tremble. She was a force to see, draped in a flowing nightdress that gently flapped with a breeze far weaker than the stormy wind that now blew, creating an uneasy disconnect between her and her earthly surroundings. The spectre's hair was fair and flowing, as if she were suspended underwater, rippling with a different timing than that of the nightdress. The separation made the viewers of this queasy and seasick, to see two detached motions acting upon one body.

The ghostly figure emitted the same glorious white light as the pool surrounding the man on the floor. In her hands, she held a large kitchen knife with white light dripping from its tip, sloped towards the floor. Anger and rage burned deeply upon her face as she looked up towards the crowd – now frozen as still as the body on the floor. She raised her empty left hand, slowly and full of purpose, and pointed directly at the young barman standing at the front of the onlookers. His blood froze in terror, and he was consumed with a sense of dread. He began to question his life choices and regret the way he had treated women. He had never been one to brag or boast, coming across to most as a likeable lad; a charmer. This had won the affections of many a young lady, whom he had become accustomed to use and abuse. Often, he strung several women along like cod on a long line. When he was done with them, he would drop them back into the water with no reasons given; just a quick cut of the line, never to be seen again. To him, women had become playthings to bring him pleasure, to be discarded when the fun was over. But of late, he found his appetite harder to satiate. The games he got those women to play behind closed doors became more and more risky and more and more violent. He would tell himself that they enjoyed it, too; that pleasure and pain were just two sides of the same coin. If they refused, that was fine – he would cut them lose and move on to someone else, who would go further and let him indulge more and more in his depravities. Now, though, it was as if the spirit of that young woman before him could see into his soul. She knew the secrets he held, his desires for those things that society saw as taboo and unnatural, and she had singled him out to be next.

Statuesque, the crowd watched on as the frightful image began to change. The light faded, and with it the image of the woman. In the sickly yellow glow of the nearby streetlight it became clear what the liquid light flowing from Murphy's neck was. It was blood. His throat had been ripped apart by a spectral blade and was left now gaping and gushing. The life had long since left the body on the floor and the heavy rain had begun to mix with and wash away the blood into a nearby drain. Once the crowd regained their senses the first to move was the barman, who ran into the pub, swiftly collected his things and left. He headed for home, never again daring to cross the threshold of that cursed former home or to venture near that fateful car park. The landlord called the emergency services, who attended the scene within minutes. Patrick Murphy was declared dead within seconds of the paramedics arriving, which the witnesses had already surmised, and the body was taken away for further investigation. The onlookers were all taken to the local police station, whereupon they were questioned at length to ascertain the exact cause of the man's death and the sequence of events that led up to it. From the extensive evidence that was gathered, and the lengthy witness statements, the local law enforcers were baffled. It all pointed to an impossibility, it seemed: to a ghost murdering a man in a car park. The local sergeant agreed with his officers that this simply could not be the case. The witnesses were questioned some more, with officers trying hard to find inconsistencies and slip-ups in their stories to blow the case open and expose the elaborate hoax and cover-up this clearly was. But each statement checked out, each one matched the other. No holes, no mistakes. There were only two possibilities: either this was the best cover-up of a murder they had ever come across, nay, there had ever been… or, impossibly, they were all telling the truth, and this was death by ghost. This, of course, could not be put down as the cause of death, so the sergeant chose to simply put a verdict of accidental death from a fight with an unknown assailant. No murder weapon was found, no other evidence of anyone being near the body – but this was explained away by the heavy rain having washed away all the evidence.

To this day, the crime sits as a cold case, never having been officially solved. But if you were to talk to those who were there that fateful night, they would tell you exactly what happened – as I have told you here, having myself been told by a witness of the haunting event. The pub shut down for some years after, before reopening as the thing the previous landlord fought so hard to avoid: a trendy gastro pub. This brought its fair share of arrogant, misogynistic male clientele. However, by this time the tale I have just recounted had become folklore, and no man ever entertained the unsolicited invitations of any strange women in the car park, and so the events of that fateful night were never repeated. However, let this be a lesson to those reading this story to treat the fairer sex with respect and dignity. And, if you ever find yourself in a restaurant with a window near the toilets that look out on the car park, don't look outside. But if you do, and you happen to see a beautiful young woman beckoning you out, you may want to question the choices you have made in your life.

THE MAN WHO WENT TO FIND HIS LUCK

And now for something completely different…

The story you are about to read is very well-known, told in many cultures around the world, in many different ways. The way I am telling it here is the way I first heard it many years ago, with a few tweaks of my own (something every good storyteller does). It is a tale examining the nature of luck, that elusive thing we all hope is with us. There are many, many folk tales that try to pick apart what luck is, for after all, folk tales are our way of trying to make sense of the world we live in.

For this story, I wanted a very light-hearted, playful vibe. In a book of unhappy endings, there has not been much of a chance to do this. The style I aimed for was a playful whimsy, and full of jokes, inspired by one of my all-time favourite writers of fiction, Terry Pratchett. He was a master of world building, description, and playful humour, and I hope I have come at least somewhere close to his witty writings. I can only dream of becoming as skilled with words as him, though.

The setting for this story is the modern day, but with old-world folklore tropes sprinkled in, such as a woman fetching water from a well. The mix of the two give this story a fantastical nature and lead to great places for humour.

What is luck? Some say you are born lucky; some believe in Lady Luck, an entity so fickle and fleeting, she is by your side one minute then gone the next; some say luck is an illusion and we forge our own path, making our own luck, seizing every chance we can, seizing the moment. Carpe Diem. Which do you believe?

Gary was in his mid-thirties. He lived at home with his parents. He was jobless and still growing (outwards). His life was an exhilarating blend of lying in until midday, playing computer games, and, if he was feeling adventurous, getting dressed and meeting his friends down the pub for a drink. There was never a dull day for Gary, the life and soul of his own party for one. Not for him the daily grind, no rat race or daily commutes. He went where he wanted, when he wanted, without the burden of children. Sure, money was, well, non-existent, but that was what the Bank of Mum and Dad was for. They said he'd have to pay them back when he got a job but, well, when would that be? If Gary had his way, that would never happen. He believed in a carefree life that was good for the soul, stress-free and easy.

One night, after a particularly hard afternoon beating random tweens from across the globe on the latest first-person shooter, he decided to slip into a pair of jeans and a T-shirt, which seemed so rigid and uncomfortable compared to his fleece pyjamas, and head down the road to the Red Lion to see his friends. Walking into the warmth of the back room with the log fire burning bright, he was met by a ripple of welcome from the people he grew up with. At school, they had been thick as thieves, revelling in playing football at playtime, messing about in class, flicking pencils across the classroom, and blowing spit wads through empty pen cases. Then, GCSEs came along. Gary found himself trying hard to keep the group together, for they all seemed to want to stay in at night to complete their homework and study. Gary's friends forgot what was important in life: having good times with the ones you care most about. However, once exams were out the way and Gary's friends had got university out of their systems, Gary was right there, back where they all met, in their hometown, waiting for them. Gary had been the one constant in their circle of friends. While everyone else moved on, used their degrees to get well-paid jobs, bought nice houses and cars, and met partners to share their lives with, Gary stayed the course, never changing, as constant as the rocks of the Earth.

Tonight, though, as he sat nursing the drink that was bought for him on the promise that the next round was on him, he studied the ring of faces. John was an accountant earning six figures. He worked hard, had a beautiful wife, a large home, kids, a nice car, and went on holiday five times a year. Ali had lucked into money, but hadn't rested on his laurels. He had followed his passions, using this money to boost his artistic dreams, helping him set up his own gallery showcasing his own and others' artwork. He had become a key player in the local art world, a respected figure and lauded as a leading innovator in art. And Dean, well, he hadn't gone to university. He had done an apprenticeship in plumbing and, by keeping his head down, being honest and hardworking, he now earned his own plumbing business, employing a dozen people. He had a fleet of vehicles, drove a high-end sports car, had the perfect two-and-a-half kids family and house in the suburbs. A self-made man, and proud of it. Then Gary looked at himself in the reflection of his half-drunk pint. He noticed the creased Star Wars t-shirt he had gotten from a charity shop, bought for him by his mum, which was getting tighter and tighter around his middle as his waistline stretched. He suddenly realised he had no job, no money, no life.

'It's not fair!' Gary proclaimed all of a sudden to his friends. 'It's not fair how you've all got good jobs, nice houses, nice cars, loved ones, the perfect life, and I'm stuck at home with my parents – the same place I've been my entire life.'

The friends stared for a second at Gary, their mouths open. They saw the sadness and upset in his eyes. They'd never seen Gary like this before. Gary was the laid back one. Gary never cared about anything. Gary was happy coasting through life, living off others, and that was fine by them. It had never hurt them, and Gary was always good for a laugh. But now, well, this was out of the blue and totally unexpected.

It was Dean who broke the silence. 'Yeah, but that's you, mate. You're the dosser, the joker. You're the one constant in our lives. You'll find something soon, mate. I'm sure you're looking out for a job.'

'No,' replied Gary. 'That's not what I mean. I don't want a job; I want my luck!' His voice was full of anger and venom, and he had a look of determination on his face.

John ventured a response. 'I'm not sure we get what you mean then. Your luck?'

John and the others looked puzzled.

Gary, looking around the group, had a realisation. An epiphany dawned like a bright and fresh new morning.

His eyes opened to the truth of his life, like a baby bird taking its first flight and realising there was a much bigger world than it thought beyond the nest. Gary now knew what he was missing: his luck!

'My luck,' Gary replied, his voice stoic and full of drive. 'The luck that should have been with me since birth. That's what I'm missing.'

Ali spoke for the three friends when he ventured the remark, 'I don't think we follow you mate…'

The friends' faces furrowed with confusion.

'The way I see it,' Gary explained, 'is that you were all given your luck by God before you were born. Look, Ali, you lucked into money to get your big break…'

'Wow, hold on mate,' Ali interjected, his voice full of upset and annoyance. 'It wasn't luck! You know that. I didn't want to lose my Granddad and Nanny in the space of a week. I've worked damn hard to use that money well and make them proud of what I have done with it, and…'

Gary butted in, waving this comment off; he hadn't finished his point. 'Yes, yes, I know mate. I'm not saying you haven't worked hard, but it was lucky you got that money. And John, you have the luck of being good with numbers. You just seem to *get* numbers, so accountancy was always on the cards for you. And Dean, nothing like a bit of nepotism to give your career a boost, aye mate?'

Dean was fuming. Yes, it was his uncle's plumbing company he had gone to work at when he left school, but he had worked bloody hard – harder than everyone else. His uncle hadn't given him an easy ride, oh no. His uncle was harder on him than any of the other apprentices. At the time, Dean hadn't realised why. It forced Dean to work hard and be the best he could be, so, when he left his uncle's company, he could set up on his own and do an amazing job of it.

'Rein your neck in, mate! My uncle worked my bollocks off! No easy ride for me! Don't you go thinking I had it easy, not like you! In your thirties, still living at home, sponging off your parents and us, the last friends you've got.'

Gary brushed this off, water off a duck's back, for he was on to something here! He had cracked the code; seen the thing everyone else had missed. 'But come on Dean, you've got to admit it was lucky you had an uncle who gave you a job, mate. I mean, it's not like you were the sharpest tool in the box at school. Even I ran rings around you!'

Dean's face glowed red. His hands slipped from his beer and fell onto his lap. Ali held him down with a well-placed hand on his shoulder and a look that told him it wasn't worth it. It would be more entertaining to just let Gary go on with his hare-brained idea.

Gary continued, 'That's it, I know what I've got to do. It's simple! I'm going to get up tomorrow, at the crack of dawn, set out into this big wide world, and find God. And when I do, I'm simply going to ask him for my missing luck. Simple!'

The others looked at each other knowingly. They knew this would never happen. Gary couldn't get up at the crack of anything before midday. And besides, many a smarter man had tried to find God. Why would Gary, a jobless, slightly overweight, thirty-something who still lived with his parents be able to do it? Ali's look had been right, thought Dean, this was well worth it. This would bring great joy and much piss-taking to their nights in the pub for many years to come, and it was worth all the drinks they'd had to buy for Gary.

So, it was settled. Gary went home just before his round (conveniently) to get packed and ready for the big adventure the next day. He then woke up at the crack of late lunch, around half one in the afternoon, realised he'd only just missed dawn by about seven hours or so, and rolled over and went back to sleep, vowing to be up in time tomorrow.

Three weeks later, Gary finally saw an hour of the morning starting with a single digit and deemed that close enough to the crack of dawn. So, pulling on some only slightly stained jeans and a T-shirt he had been saving on his floor-drobe for this very day, he left the house. He then returned, as he realised he'd forgotten his rucksack. Once this was firmly on his back, he left on his big adventure once more. It was about at the end of the street when he realised he was still wearing his slippers and had to trek all the way back home to change into his hiking boots. As he was leaving once again, and whilst he was near the house, he realised it was about lunchtime, so he took advantage of the endless supply of food in his parents' pantry and had some lunch before setting off for a third time. This time he was off for real!

Gary travelled far, he travelled near, he travelled there, he travelled here. Having your dad's free bus pass helped no end! He didn't look that different to his dad and the under-paid, overworked bus drivers, on the whole, couldn't care less that he wasn't his 66-year-old father and just let him on. Somewhere near the south of the country, Gary came to the edge of a forest. The trees weren't that big, and it looked relatively new, despite having been there since around 1066. Gary had no idea where he was. Geography had never been the best subject for Gary at school; he just thought it was lessons in colouring in. He tried really hard to stay in the lines but didn't pay attention to words, labels, and keys on the pictures. Apparently, they were called maps. Who'd have known? Well, Gary would have, if only he'd bothered to listen in class.

It was then, as he was walking at top speed into the deep, dark forest (Gary was never one to take advice from the stories he was told as a kid), a wolf spotted him. First a deep, dark forest, now a wolf – you'd think he was in a fairy story or something!

'Man!' cried the wolf in a weak, drawn-out growl. 'Man, where are you going in such a rush, Man?' asked the wolf.

Gary stopped and looked. There, sure enough, was a large dog – or at least that was what Gary thought. He didn't pay much attention to the nature programmes his dad watched. The large dog (wolf), Gary noticed, was nothing but skin and bones, worn to a whisper. He'd seen fatter skeletons at Halloween! That reminded him, when was Halloween? And did the clocks go backwards or forwards around that time? He could never remember. And, hang on, how come that large dog could talk?

'Oh, hello!' replied Gary in a very surprised tone. 'How can I help you Mr Talking Dog?'

Well, it is rather weird to come across a talking dog, and Gary had no previous experience in this field (or the next field; it was his first time in any field) so he just chose to be polite and speak back.

'I'm not a dog,' replied the raspy voice. 'I am a wolf!'

'A wolf?' Gary was a bit confused. He seemed to remember seeing something, sometime, somewhere, about there no longer being wolves in Britain. Had they been reintroduced? They'd brought back beavers, he remembered, which he thought was a damn good idea (he was proud of that pun in his head). He'd laughed at the innuendo when he saw the headline: 'Beavers are Back!'

'Yes, a wolf. You know, big and bad and all that?' The wolf meekly tried to bare his teeth, but was lacking the energy to do this with any conviction.

'You don't look very big and bad,' replied Gary, looking the shaggy creature up and down. 'You look half-starved. What's up?'

The wolf smiled a half-smile, for it was the first time anyone had paid him any heed or kindness. Normally people just ran away from him or, at worst, come at him with an axe when he was trying to sleep off a good meal. 'I am hungry.'

Gary gazed at the bag of bones before him. 'You don't say?'

Choosing to ignore this sarcasm, the wolf continued. 'I have not eaten in weeks! I have found no food to eat, no animals to hunt. I am at a loss what to do. But you, man – you have not answered my question. Where are you going in such a hurry?'

'Oh, yes,' Gary replied, vaguely remembering this question just before his mind trundled down the tracks towards questions about Halloween. 'Yes, erm, well, I was born without my luck, and I have decided to track down God himself and ask him directly what he has done with my luck and where it might be.'

'That's ambitious, and a bit far-fetched,' the wolf began. 'You're off to find God, but you looked surprised to come across a talking wolf… never mind.' The wolf continued, 'Well, would you be able to ask God a question for me, if you find him?'

Gary stroked his chin. 'Well, I can try and remember, but I wouldn't hold out much hope. I once forgot to put my trousers on when going on a night out.' Gary wasn't great at remembering, but he didn't really care. 'Go on though, try me. I'll see what I can do.'

The wolf didn't look very hopeful, but proceeded to ask the question anyway. 'When you find God,' he rasped, 'can you ask him what I can eat? Surely, he must have an answer for me.'

'Well,' came the response, 'if I remember I can ask but, like I say, I've got the memory of a goldfish – which actually have a really good memory. I saw that on a YouTube video. So maybe I actually have the memory of a fly…

'Anyway, what were we talking about?' Gary looked at the wolf, with its forlorn expression. 'Oh yes! Asking God what you can eat. Got it!'

And with that, Gary resumed his epic quest to find God and ask him where his luck was – with not even a wave let alone a 'Goodbye' to that poor wolf, who just shrugged and accepted his fate.

Gary continued to travel far, he travelled near, he travelled there, he travelled here. After many bus rides; a rather exciting, but vomit-filled, ferry ride; and a long walk, he found himself in a foreign land where the people spoke a foreign language. A language that spoke of love and romance. Gary tried his best to communicate, by speaking loudly and slowly with a slight Chinese accent (even though this land was most definitely not China). He was amazed, though, when the people he spoke to rolled their eyes and spoke back to him in near-perfect English. Very convenient, he thought.

At length, he came to a rolling countryside with quaint farmhouses and villages dotted here and there, and the odd chateau nestled high on a hill. He spent some time in one of these villages, using his parents' credit card to full effect, staying at a delightful Airbnb above a *boulangerie* (whatever one of those was, he thought). Every morning, he was awoken early by the baker with his tray like always, the same old bread and rolls to sell. Every morning just the same, since the morning he first came to this poor provincial town… Wait – no, that was a Disney song. Never mind, he thought. He was hungry, and he wanted one of those pan-things with chocolate in it!

One morning, he checked out of the flat he had hired and strolled through the town speaking the lingo like a native (or so he thought).

'*Bonjour, bonjour, bonjour, bonjour, bonjour!*' (It was all he could say)

While soaking in the sun at the edge of the town, he noticed a young woman sat on the well. She was brown of hair, fair of face, and had a stack of books next to her. Again, Gary had a niggling feeling that this all seemed oddly familiar. He shook his head, and continued to walk by, pursing his lips together and whistling a merry tune. He suddenly realised that pretty young woman sat on the well was crying. A fat, bell-bottomed tear rolled down her face. She sobbed and began to speak to Gary,

'Man, oh cheerful man?' (Gary noticed how good her English was, and was surprised she knew *he* was English, since he'd been speaking the local lingo so fluently.) 'Where are you going to, Man?'

Gary replied out of politeness, 'Oh, erm, *bonjour.*' He beamed, feeling like a local. 'I'm Gary, nice to meet you.'

He felt awkward. He could clearly see this woman was upset, and upset women made him uneasy. He didn't know what to say or do, so he was always just super polite and tried to keep the conversation brief.

'I'm going to find God to find out why he hasn't given me my luck. Lovely to meet you. Bye.'

He then hung his head and began to shuffle away when the woman began to talk.

'Bugger!' he muttered under his breath. He might have to stay and talk *emotions*! His worst nightmare!

'You're going to find God?' the woman began, with hope now in her voice. 'If you find him, could you ask him a question for me and tell me what he says on your way back home?'

Gary wanted a quick end to the conversation. It would have been so easy to say 'No,' and 'Good day,' and shuffle off, never to see her again. But there was something about this woman that made him stay. She had a look, not of a pin-up beauty but of the woman who could warm your heart on the coldest of days with her smile. Her eyes were the deepest blue; a blue so deep you could dive into them and sink to the bottom. The more Gary looked upon her the more beautiful she became. She had a beauty that only revealed itself to those that took the time to look and talk.

Gary didn't give a verbal answer, just a distant look and grunt. The woman took this as a yes, and began to ask him the question, trying to ignore the drool now coming from the corner of Gary's mouth.

'If you find God, could you ask him why I am so sad?' The woman looked hopeful and, with no immediate response forthcoming, she continued. 'I have a pretty perfect life. I live with my father (he's an inventor), I've got a secure job, and I've saved up for a deposit on a house, but I just don't know…' She looked mournfully into the middle distance. 'I feel sad all the time and just don't know why.'

Wanting desperately to avoid emotion-talk, despite this woman's beauty, Gary responded. 'When I find God, I will ask him why you are so sad and let you know when I come back this way. Now, I hope you don't mind, but God won't find himself, so I must be off!'

Gary shuffled off out the village and down the road, head down and berating himself for the way he ended that conversation.

God won't find himself? he thought. *Of course he will! He just has to look down and there he is, found! And even if you take it in the spiritual meaning of 'finding yourself', then of course, God will have found himself. If he hasn't, then everyone else on their spiritual journey holiday in a yurt in a field in Gloucestershire taking baths in a barrel hasn't got a chance!*

Gary travelled far, he travelled near, he travelled there, he travelled here. South and east he went. His preferred mode of transport was trains. He watched as the landscapes rolled by, changing hour by hour from large, mostly flat lands covered in crops, to hills that gave way to snow-capped mountains. He traversed clifftops and rolled on through a mountain range, taking it all in whilst living his best life in comfort and style. His father clearly hadn't realised what Gary was doing and, well, whilst the card continued to work, Gary continued to spend. But just like with the trains, he couldn't ride this out for long. After all, he had no luck. Gary found proof of this when, in a valley far from anywhere, beneath towering mountains, he was approached by a train steward.

'*Mi scusi, signore*,' they began, before seeing the puzzled look on Gary's face and converting to English. 'Sir, I am sorry to say that your card was declined when you purchased your ticket. This was not noticed until the train had left. We will not be able to take you any further.'

And with that, Gary was escorted off the train and left all alone on a tiny strip of concrete with a single sign he could not read.

Great, Gary thought. *What now?*

He looked around and saw a path leading out of the station and along a crystal-clear mountain river that curved its way through the valley, having taken its time over many thousands of years to forge its own path – and the valley itself. Gary felt a pull in that direction and, trusting his luck (not that he had any, of course), followed it.

He walked upstream, as it seemed to him that if God was to be found he would be high up. Gary came to a most beautiful place. Willow trees bowed low over the river, their lush green branches in full leaf and lapping at the water. The sun sparkled and played on the ripples and flows of the stream. The sun glistened on the snow crowning the mountains in front of him. At that moment, that perfect moment, Gary breathed in deeply. Life, right there, right then, was perfect, he thought. Nothing else mattered for him just then.

'Man,' came a whisper upon the breeze. 'Man, where are you going to, Man?' The voice floating through the air and into Gary's ears. It spoke to him like a warm summer's breeze, but with the threat of a summer storm on the horizon.

Gary turned around in all directions to see who had called him. He saw nobody.

'Hello,' Gary said. 'Erm, hello? Who said that?'

'It was me,' the whisper said, coming from a tree behind Gary.

Gary spun around to be confronted with a willow tree, much the same as the rest. But this poor soul was bare and barren of leaf. In the height of summer as it was, not a single green leaf crowned this mighty tree.

'Tell me, if you would be so kind, where you are going? You look both lost and found and seem both in a hurry and altogether at a stop.'

Gary was amazed. *A talking tree,* he thought to himself, before realising he'd already spoken to a wolf on this journey, so this wasn't that alarming. In fact, he found it rather entertaining, Entertaining…

There goes that bell again, Gary thought. But this particular talking-tree train of thought barely had time to leave the station when the actual tree, with lichen that looked awfully like a beard, began to talk once more, prompting him.

'Oh yes, sorry Mr Tree With a Beard.' Since Gary didn't know this tree's name, this seemed a polite way to address him. 'I am searching the world to find God. You see, he has forgotten to give me my luck, and so I intend to ask where it might be and if I can have it and start living my life.' Looking up into the branches, away from the main, face-like trunk, Gary asked, 'Tell me, if you would, why you are so barren with your leaves when your friends are so lush? Surely willow trees growing next to a mountain river would all be in the best of health.' Even Gary knew this.

Gary heard what sounded like a sigh as the breeze whistled through the branches of the bearded tree, before the tree continued. 'Alas, you would think I would be in the rudest of health, but, for some reason, my roots cannot find the water and drink the cool mountain tears. If you find God, would you ask him what is stopping my roots from drinking from the river?'

'Of course,' replied Gary. 'If I remember, that is. I've already met a starving wolf who wants to know what he can eat and a beautiful young woman who wants to know why she is so sad all the time. But, if I remember, I'll add your question to the list. Is that OK?'

Gary's faced beamed at the face-like trunk. He loved trees, and the thought of helping one out gave him great joy.

The tree lifted its branches, like a person rolling their shoulders back and standing tall. 'That would be a true act of kindness, the likes of which a tree like me has not seen for an age. Men of this world only ever come with axe and saw, chopping and biting at us, using us trees for tools, fuel, furniture, or nothing more than mulch!' The tree could feel his sap rising. 'Men only ever use trees for their own end, but you,' the tree's branches fell and shivered, as if relaxing, 'you, Man, are different. You care, and for that, on behalf of all trees, I thank you.'

Gary bowed low, feeling honoured and, knowing his time with this most noble of trees was ended, he said his goodbyes and headed off. This encounter would live long (ish) in his memory as a most magical and special of meetings.

Heading upwards, Gary climbed a mountain pass. Higher and higher he climbed, until the air grew thin, and it was hard to breathe. He turned and looked behind him. Below, he spied the mountain pass he had scaled, silver in the late afternoon sunlight, winding down to meet the river below. He could see the willow trees that lined the water, now a mass of green with one noticeable brown spot amongst them. The rest of the valley sprawled out before him. He was so high, he felt he was on top of the world and that he could touch the very sky itself. This was, Gary thought, surely as close to heaven as any mortal man could get. He breathed in the thin, bitter cold mountain air and smiled, closing his eyes to feel the full force of the experience.

When he opened his eyes, he noticed a cave next to him. That wasn't there before, was it? He hadn't noticed it, but now he felt different. He felt more, well, alive. The hole in the mountain wasn't 'a nasty, dirty, wet hole, filled with the ends of worms and an oozy smell, nor yet a dry, bare, sandy hole with nothing in it to sit down on or to eat,' (Gary hadn't read much but he had read *The Hobbit*, so the reference was not lost on him). This hole shone with bright white light, and ethereal choral music drifted out from within. Gary felt his feet being pulled towards it. He felt like now was the time, and his entire life had been heading to this moment. His mind and body were open and ready for this meeting.

At the end of a bright white passage the cave opened up into a cathedral-like space. The light was so bright it was hard to see anything. What Gary did see was an enormous throne, shimmering in white and a thousand colours all at the same time, as if the light was radiating from it and being split into its base colours all at the same time. Its pearlescence was beyond beauty. And there, sat upon the throne, circled by angelic figures in the air, was an old man; older than time itself, Gary thought. This man was dressed in a simple but dazzling white robe from head to toe. His long, white beard fell like a waterfall to the ground before him. Then Gary noticed his eyes. They were both blue, and green, and brown, all at the same time. His face was that of an old man but had the look of youth etched upon it in a beautiful counterbalance, giving this man an ageless feel. He was every man Gary had ever seen. And more, he was also every woman, for as Gary looked closer, he noticed feminine features: soft cheek bones, a delicate smile, all merged into one. Within this face Gary saw the entire human race: white, black, brown, young, old, man, woman, framed by the white beard and long, full, white hair that sat upon his shoulders. Gary knew this was God. He fell to his knees at once in reverence, awe and fear, bowing his head low to the ground in respect.

'Come, come now,' boomed a voice, which seemed eerily familiar to Gary. 'There is no need for that! I should be bowing to you.'

Gary looked confused at this statement and also at the fact he realised that God sounded like Mufasa.

'You, my creation, have travelled far and wide to seek me out – and, after what you have experienced in the valley and on the mountain pass, you have found me.'

No, hold on, thought Gary, God's voice was Morgan Freeman's voice!

'You have experienced the true beauty of this world and its true majesty, and you have learnt to appreciate it. This brought you closer to the divine; closer to me. Only by experiencing this can you commune with me.' God bowed to Gary and said, 'Now, you have a question or four for me, yes?'

Maybe it was Liam Neeson, Gary thought. But it was probably not very respectful to ask God to say, 'I will find you and I will kill you,' just so he could be certain.

'God, oh mighty one, I have come with a question from me, and three questions from the wonderful creations within your world,' Gary began.

'Ask yours first,' replied God, 'and then we shall see about the others.'

No, thought Gary, *it's Darth Vader… but hold on, that's the same guy who plays Mufasa!* Still mulling this over in his head, Gary began to ask his question.

'With the greatest of respects, oh great one, creator of all, I think that maybe, just maybe, you have made a mistake.' Gary's heart was pounding, almost bursting from his chest.

'A mistake, you say?' questioned God, now sounding like Gandalf.

'Erm, yes,' replied Gary, now looking at his feet and shuffling. 'You see, my friends have all got money and families and are happy and they had loads of luck, but…' Gary faltered before continuing, '… but, they've had luck to do all that. I've got no money, and nobody to love me. I'm lonely, broke, and bored. I think, again, with the greatest of respect Ganda – erm, God –that you may have forgotten to give me my luck.'

There was silence for a moment before God responded with a wry smile on his face. 'Oh yes,' he said as he stroked his beard in an all-knowing kind of way, 'I remember now! Your luck. Yes. I seem to remember, as I was handing out everyone's luck before they were sent to Earth, yours slipped out of my fingers.' He paused for dramatic effect.

'Of course, that makes sense,' Gary acknowledged. 'It was an accident. A mighty being, the most mighty of all, the kindest, most benevolent of them all, would not simply *forget* to give me my luck. This makes total sense!'

'Total sense,' came the voice of James Earl Jones, dripping like treacle into Gary's ear.

Gary continued, after a brief moment's pause to drink in that sweet, sweet voice. 'So, if it slipped from your fingers, where is it now?' Gary looked up expectantly, like a puppy waiting for a treat, his eyes wide open.

'Your luck,' explained Morgan Freeman, 'is out there in the world somewhere. You are different to most in that you will have to find your own luck. Yes, you will have to seize every opportunity that comes your way. Be on your guard, though,' Ian McKellen warned, 'for that luck of yours is a slippery beast. It has already slipped from my fingers! When you find a piece of it, grab it there and then. Don't let it go! *Carpe diem*. Do you understand?'

Gary looked confused. 'Yes, all except the bit about the big fish.'

It was now God's turn to look confused, but only for a brief moment. '*Carpe diem*. It's Latin for "seize the day". Understand now?'

'Oh,' exclaimed Gary, his cheeks flushing red. 'Yes, I knew that, of course.' He bowed several times whilst walking backwards. 'Thank you, mighty one, thank you, thank you, thank you.' Gary did feel like he was overdoing it somewhat but, hey, this was God, right? He deserved all this praise. 'That is exactly what I needed to hear, then…'

He stopped. He suddenly remembered the large dog, the beautiful girl and the tree with a beard. 'Oh, shoot, sorry.' He had actually said a stronger word than 'shoot', but in the presence of God, no curse words can be said. This would be blasphemous, so God came with his own built-in filter, which was very handy. Gary didn't actually notice though. He began to explain what had happened on his journey, the people and things that he had met, and the questions they had for him. God duly obliged with the answers to their conundrums and saw Gary on his way.

Gary left that cave beaming like the sun. He had actually met God! He had spoken with the great almighty himself, and now knew where his luck was. He had been right this whole time! He hadn't had his luck, for it was out there waiting for him to find it. As he stood on the side of that mountain, looking at the world outstretched ahead of him, he was excited for the adventure before him. He took his first step on this new life he would lead, his first step down the mountain to find his luck. As he did, he glanced back to the cave to find it had gone. No bright lights, no choral music; just a collection of boulders in a vaguely cave shape. Had he dreamed it all? He couldn't have, surely. Well, the only way to find out was to test what God had said and to strike out and find his luck!

After travelling far, travelling near, travelling there, and travelling here, Gary came to the bottom of the mountain, alongside that river of crystal-clear, ice-cold water, lined with willow trees dancing in the summer breeze.

'Man,' came that whispered voice. 'Man, did you find God, Man?'

Turning to the dead-looking tree with a beard, Gary smiled and said, 'Yes, I did! I found God, up there on the mountainside.' He pointed to where he had just journeyed from. 'I found God and he told me my luck was in this world, and I was to seek it out and seize it when I find it.'

'And what of me,' asked the tree, full of hope. 'What of my roots not being able to drink from that stream?'

'Oh yes, I did remember,' replied Gary, happy with himself that he had. 'I asked, and God said you have a hoard of gold beneath your roots. It is massive, worth more than any other treasure in this world. What you need,' he explained, 'is for somebody to dig it out for you so you may push your roots into the damp soil beneath the stream, drink long and hard, and live!'

The whole tree lifted in hope and began to speak once more. 'Man, would you be able to do that task for me? There is an old, discarded shovel resting by the bank over there.' The tree's branches seemed to sway in the direction of the old shovel. 'I'm sure it won't take lo…'

But the tree was cut short by Gary and his reply. 'Sorry, I would love to help you, but I have my entire life to live and all my luck just waiting for me to find it out there in the wide, wide world. I haven't got time to be digging out treasure from beneath your roots. It would take me all day!' And with that, continued his journey.

'But Man,' called the tree in whispers, 'please, think of the…'

But once more his voice was cut off by Gary's response. 'I'm off to find my luck, sorry!' And he skipped off, full of bounce and enthusiasm, down the road.

Gary continued his journey, turning now towards home, travelling far and near, there and here, west and north, until he found himself once again in that poor, provincial town. Not a lot had happened since he had left. There was some talk about a local hunter with girls swooning after him, but Gary had no time for that gossip and nonsense.

He did, however, run into that bookish beauty, sitting by the well.

'Man,' she called after him, 'Man, did you find God, Man?'

Gary paused and looked at her. She wasn't crying this time, thankfully. He couldn't take another awkward conversation like last time, no matter how perfect she seemed otherwise. 'I did,' he answered, 'I found God and he told me my luck was out here in the world for me to find. Wealth and happiness within my grasp. And, would you believe it,' Gary explained about the tree and the gold and how he hadn't possibly got time to dig all that up, all that gold and…

'Did you ask about me,' the girl interrupted, full of hope, 'did you ask what I'm missing in my life?'

'Oh, yes,' Gary beamed at the fact he'd remembered, 'and he said this. He said you are missing someone to share your life with.'

'But I have that; my father.' The girl looked confused.

Gary explained what God had meant. 'No, no, someone to have and to hold, till death do you part and all that jazz, you know?'

The girl understood. She then looked at Gary. She saw that, yes, he was a bit soft around the middle, and he had seen better days, but this man had kindness in his eyes and wasn't too bad to look at. *Maybe, just maybe,* she thought.

'My father is cooking his famous beef bourguignon tonight, if you would like to join us. We have guest quarters in the annex. You could stay and rest a while, recover from your long journey.' The girl looked hopeful. 'We could, maybe, get to know each other; go for a coffee; chat. Just a thought.' She smiled a coy, shy smile, half looking at the ground. At that moment Gary's heart began to beat hard against his chest. Things began to swell in various places.

His mouth opened to say yes, when he remembered what God had said. His luck was out there to find and, well, as lovely as this woman was, he needed to find his luck first and foremost.

'That sounds like a lovely idea, it really does,' Gary said, 'but I really must get on and find my luck.' And with that, he was gone, not even a second glance back to the only woman that had ever made his heart flutter like a butterfly.

Once more, Gary travelled far and near, there and here, on that vomit-inducing ferry, and up to the edge of that rather new-looking forest where he once again came across the emaciated wolf.

'Man,' came the drawn-out growl from the wolf. 'Man, did you find God, Man?'

Gary stopped and saw this large dog was even thinner than before, if that was even possible. 'Yes,' Gary chirped with glee, 'yes I did, and he told me my luck was out in the world and I was to find it, seizing every piece of it I could to make my fortune and find my happiness. And then, well, you'll never believe this, but…'

And Gary explained about everything that had happened. He explained about the hoard of gold under the tree and how he hadn't possibly got the time to spend digging that out; he had to find his luck. He then explained about the girl, that most beautiful of women, the only woman ever to have made his heart flutter, and how, despite the lovely invite back to her house for tea, he had to continue on in the hope he'd find his luck.

After hearing all of this the wolf asked, 'And what of me? What should I eat?'

'Oh yes,' Gary grinned, pleased he had remembered to ask God. 'You, good dog – erm, no, wolf, right? Anyway, you, you are to eat the next foolish man to come your way,

God said. I pity that man, I really do,' sighed Gary, looking at the wolf. 'You may be nearly dead with hunger, but you've still got a mighty pair of gnashers on you, and those claws!' He drew in his breath and whistled. 'They could rip you to shreds in seconds. Anyway, enough of that, I've got my luck to find. Bye.'

The wolf may have only been a wolf, but he knew a foolish man when he saw one. He looked Gary up and down and thought on the things he had said: the treasure he had passed up on, the life he had not even given a chance to. And, well, that night, the wolf's belly was full for the first time in a very long time, and this story came to a rather abrupt end.

So, dear reader, what can we take from this tale of foolishness, of laziness, and of a search for a quick fix? For certain, we can agree that there are no quick fixes in life and that we must stay alert to the signs of luck. Sometimes, even when lady luck smacks you around the face with a wet fish, you may be so distracted by other things you won't even see it or smell it, but you'll wonder for hours who brought the tuna salad in to work as the place stinks! Your luck can be right in front of your eyes, but you might be too short-sighted to even smell it.

Carpe diem.

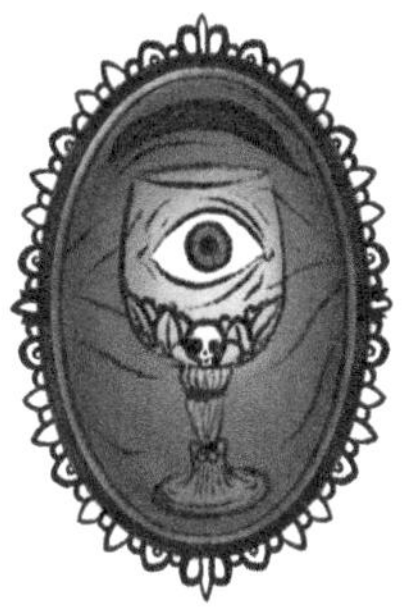

THE SOLDIER AND DEATH

This is the story that started it all for me. The first story I ever told to my class of children and the first story I ever told to a live adult audience. It was a story I first saw play out on my old CRT TV, tucked away in the corner of the living room, hungry for 50p pieces, the original pay-to-play. It was Christmas and, in the Radio Times, I had spotted a show called The StoryTeller. *I was a huge fan of* Labyrinth, *the beautifully made cult classic fantasy by the geniuses at Jim Henson's Creature Workshop, and I had watched through my fingers in awe and wonder at the wonderfully dark and magical* The Dark Crystal, *so I was very excited to see a series by this amazing studio coming to TV. I remember watching, eyes and mouth wide open, as the delightful John Hurt told his story to the brilliantly puppeteered dog that lay beside him and the blazing fireplace. Of course, the storyteller by the fire is the oldest of clichés, but it never fails to draw you in. These stories were interlaced with live action, a mix of actors (such as Bob Peck and Sean Bean) and puppet creatures. The heady mix was magical and captured my 8-year-old imagination and has never let go. It was this series that I give credit to for me eventually becoming a storyteller.*

All the episodes in the first series were based on European folk tales, collected by the brilliant storyteller Ben Haggerty, although he was sadly never credited for this. By far, the standout story for me, though, was The Soldier and Death. *The story hit hard, dealing with a very weighty subject for a boy who had never experienced loss before, except that of a beloved pet. I truly believe this one story has shaped my entire view on death, causing me to be very pragmatic about it, accepting it is very sad but also a much-needed part of the world. Without it, living would not be as fun as it is. Life is a gift; death is inevitable.*

The story as it appears here is very similar to the version you will see onscreen and the version Ben Haggarty still tells to this day, although there are, of course, tweaks and changes to make this story my own, such as the second beggar's story and the reference to the previous story in this book, The Man Who Went to Find His Luck. *I like trying to link my stories in some way within my books. I have also adapted this as an hour-long storytelling set, which I have performed across the country at storytelling clubs, titled:* Devils, Death, and a Hessian Sack.

I won't say too much more about this and will let you discover the magic of the story that started it all for me, and opened my eyes to the wonder of an unhappily ever after.

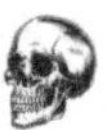

Our story starts right where all good stories start: at the beginning. Well, this beginning is also an end, but an end of a story – that is not for telling now. This story begins with a soldier, leaving the army, to begin his new life of freedom. But where does he go? All this soldier has known is service. He joined the army at 16 and now, a man in his mid-life, the army was all he'd ever known. Waking up with the dawn, drills, training, service. And then the wars, the battles, the fighting. Friends he'd made, like brothers to him, now gone: fallen on the field of battle, some surviving and getting out through injury, some forever sleeping, their time on this Earth over. The soldier had seen more than his fair share of death and delivered death to more than his fair share of people. He had been good – no, not just good, *exceptional* – at what he did. The soldier delivered death coolly and effectively to those who fought against him. But now he was leaving death behind, on the fields of slaughter. These wars were made by the men in charge, sending their puppets into battle. The soldier was a weapon, wielded by the powerful; a blunt instrument to batter back enemy lines, to claim land and territory. Lives didn't matter to those men; only land and victory in arms. The soldier was out of this, and he was glad.

He had been a member of the King's Royal Hussars. This badge he still wore with pride and in memory of his fallen comrades, upon the left shoulder of his great coat, which he had been allowed to keep, along with his roll mat to sleep on. He was gifted his boots, also, although they had seen better (and worse) days, and were worn almost through in places. These were the days before army pensions, before thank yous to those who had given the best years of their life in service. No military pension, no benefits of any kind for this soldier. Just a handshake, a shilling and three dried biscuits for the road. When this story starts, though, he had spent his shilling and was down to no more than his three dried biscuits. The soldier walked wearily along a winding road to who-knows-where, where he came across a beggar. The soldier stopped and marvelled at what this old boy was doing. The old beggar was nought but skin and bones, dressed head to toe in rags with a scrap of a mongrel curled up beside him. The dog slept soundly in the late morning sunshine of the fine summer's day, soaking in the warmth whilst his owner played a merry tune upon his battered old fiddle. This fiddle was the only thing the beggar owned; the soldier could tell. Even the dog seemed to be his own master, belonging to not the beggar; not to anyone. But the fiddle – that old, beaten, violin – half the strings broken or frayed upon the bow, knocks and dents in the body: that was the beggar's. He'd had it since he was a boy and knew every imperfection. His fingers had worn grooves where they fell for the note positions. This, by no means, meant the beggar was a good fiddler. But he could hold a tune made of a merry beat and notes that soared and lifted the soul.

The soldier stopped and listened. He had barely heard any music for many a year. In war, the playing of music was forbidden, should it give away your position to the enemy. Now, this music, as basic and rustic as it was, made the soldier's heart leap and his lips purse together. From between his chapped lips came a sound, one that he had not made since he was a boy, playing in the fields, in a time he had forgotten. The whistle that wheezed from his lips had all the right notes for the beggar's tune, just never really in the same order. But on that fine morning, when the soldier had not a care in the world, at that moment, it didn't matter. Life didn't matter. All that mattered was the fiddler, the whistler, and the music they made. One couldn't whistle and the other couldn't fiddle but that made no odds to either man.

When the tune was over and done, the soldier brought his hands together hard and fast. 'Bravo! Bravo!' he shouted. 'What a fine and merry tune, the like of which I have not heard in an age. Thank you.' The soldier beamed at the beggar with delight.

'Thank you,' came the cracked and croaky voice of the beggar in reply, 'was it worth a farthing?' Taking the bow in his fiddle hand, he reached out his palm hoping for it to be crossed with silver. Even bronze would be welcomed.

'Yes,' came the soldier's response, 'it is worth many farthings, many indeed, for an old soldier whose ears have not heard such jolly song in far too long.' His expression then dulled. 'But, alas,' he said with sunken face, 'I have spent all my money.' The soldier looked at the ground in shame and sadness, as this poor old fiddler deserved something for his song; something more than just praise and a round of applause for a lifetime of practice and work. His hands fell into his pocket as he hung his head in shame, and they fell upon those three dried biscuits – all that was left to show off his lifetime of service, besides the coat they were in and the scraps of leather masquerading as boots on his feet. 'Here,' the soldier said with excitement, 'here, you can have this.' He presented the beggar with one of the biscuits. 'Yes, it's old and dry and may not taste great but,' the soldier smiled, 'it is something, and better than nothing. I have but three of these, the only things I have in this world apart from the clothes on my back. But you, good sir, you are more than worthy of one of these, and I am deeply sorry I cannot give you more.' His voice trailed off and his head bowed in shame once more as he realised how meagre this offering actually was.

The old beggar looked upon this offering, looked upon the soldier's face, and, with a lifetime of wisdom knocking around his head, realised the significance of this offering. Men with more in their lives would take this as an insult – a biscuit for their time – but the soldier had as much as the beggar:

nothing. Nothing but these dried biscuits, and the beggar knew the sacrifice the soldier was making, and he smiled.

'Thank you,' came the beggar's cracked voice. 'Thank you for your kindness. You're a good man.' He motioned. 'A good man who deserves more in this world. This world has kicked you down and left you in the gutter with me, but you deserve more. For a start,' the beggar continued, 'you deserve a better whistle. Now, thank you, and be on with your journey, wherever your feet may carry you.' And with that the beggar bowed to the soldier and motioned his hand down the lane that snaked on into the distance.

The soldier began to walk, his tired legs carrying his aching body ever onward, ever forward to a place he knew of not. As he walked, the tune the beggar had given him played on loop in his head. Round and around it went, until the soldier unconsciously pursed his lips together and began to blow out a wheeze and a whistle. But this time – this time, friends – this time there was no wheeze to speak of. The tuneless whistle had gone and, in its place, came a whistle like diamonds and rubies! The ruby whistle was clean and sharp, like the robin welcoming in the promise of a warm summer's day. The whistle soared in the high notes, roared in the low notes, and seemed to shake the branches of the trees with its beauty and force. All that heard it for miles around found their mouths curling up at the ends, and the day suddenly seemed brighter. The soldier marvelled at the gift the old beggar had given him. He blew, and blew, and blew, as he began to skip with a new-found sense of wonder for the world. This was a gift that lifted his soul and gave him a sense of purpose, and for that he was more than glad.

Whistling away down the road, the soldier came at length, sometime in the early afternoon, to a second beggar.

This old man beckoned to the traveller to take the weight off his feet, and to sit and listen a while whilst the beggar regaled him with a story. This beggar was a storyteller and, as it is with any good storyteller, knew just the right story to tell for the audience that bent their ear and listened. The soldier – having spent a lifetime only hearing tragic tales of the death of his friends in war, and having only sad stories to tell himself – gladly sat, opened his ears and his mind, and let the old storyteller weave his words and tell his tale. The soldier listened as the teller of tales told of a man who went to find his luck, of the man's stupidity, and how his drive to find his missing luck blinded him to the bounty that lay in front of him, before he met a rather sticky end. The soldier sat for a while in thought as the storyteller ended the story. The narrative and themes resonated to the core of the soldier. Now it was time for him to find his luck, he thought, but he was to learn the lessons of this story. The soldier was determined to seize every opportunity now he was a free man; free from orders and service. Realising what he had been given, the gift of knowledge from this story, the soldier brought his hands together and applauded the beggar.

'Bravo, bravo, bravo!' He beamed with happiness. He could not remember when he had been this happy and this driven to strike out in the world and begin his new life.

'Worth a farthing?' came the response from the storyteller.

'More,' replied the soldier, 'but, alas, I have spent all my money, and I am down to nothing but two dried biscuits.' Of course, the soldier thought, he was going to share these biscuits with the storyteller, as he had with the fiddler, for that was only fair and just, was it not? Reaching into his pocket, the soldier produced one of the biscuits and offered it to the beggar. 'Here, please, take one of my biscuits. It's not much, but it is all I have, and you deserve it for that wonderful story that has stirred my heart and given me a new focus and hope in this world.'

The beggar, as with the last, saw the size of this gesture for what it really was, and smiled as he took the crumbling cookie from the soldier's hand. 'You're a good man,' said the storyteller, 'who deserves a bit more luck in your life. Thank you, and may the road carry you well to your final destination.' And with that, he bowed and motioned down the dusty road.

Setting off once more, the soldier whistled his ruby whistle whilst his head span with the story: the chances spurned, the mistakes made, the opportunities missed. He vowed not to make those same mistakes. And, as luck would have it, the soldier came to a third beggar alongside the dusty road.

This old boy was worn to a whisper; nothing but skin and bones, barely held together. He sat at a table playing with a pack of cards. These cards had seen better days. They were frayed and worn, but much-loved. The soldier took a moment to watch and was rewarded with things he had never seen. He looked on in wonder as the beggar's bony fingers shuffled the cards, cut the pack, ruffled the two halves together, and split the pack once more. Then he dealt them onto the rickety old table. First to touch the wood was an ace of spades, closely followed by the two of spades, the three of spades, and so on, and so forth, finishing with the king of spades. A perfect straight flush. This was impossible, thought the soldier – to have shuffled the pack so much, and yet still deal such a perfect hand. He then watched on as those old digits scooped up the deck and began moving and shuffling the cards in ways that made the soldier's brain hurt. Splits, ruffles, and more. And again, once more, the beggar dealt another perfect hand, this time starting with the ace of hearts and running through to the king.

'Amazing!' cheered the soldier with excitement. 'Truly magical.'

As with the past two beggars, an old hand stretched out and the beggar asked, 'Worth a farthing?'

And as before, the soldier answered, 'More, but alas, I have spent the shilling I was given.' His hand fell into his pocket and onto the last of the dried biscuits. He pulled it out and snapped it in half, looking at it. He went to offer a half to the beggar, knowing he would need the other half to eat for himself later. But it didn't seem right, did it? Oh no, it didn't seem right, to give this talented old soul less than the others. Besides, the story that had been gifted to the soldier by the previous beggar was running loud in his head. Could this be an opportunity?

He held out both halves of the biscuit and said, 'Here. It's not much, but I have this biscuit you can have. You are in more need of it than me, and besides, you deserve it for the magic I just witnessed.'

The beggar bowed with humility and took the biscuit halves with both hands. 'Thank you,' he said, 'thank you, kind stranger. You are a good man who deserves to not be so down on his luck.' Picking up the worn old pack of playing cards, he offered them to the soldier. 'Please, take these cards, and may they never lose for you, bringing you all the luck in the world.'

The soldier knew he could not take these cards from the beggar. Begging with these wonderful cards was all the beggar had in his life. Without them, how would he get money or food?

'Respectfully, I cannot take these,' replied the soldier, 'for these are yours and you need them. But thank you, it was a very kind offer.'

'Nonsense,' snapped the beggar. His prunish face wrinkled even more and his voice became stern. 'Did you not learn anything from that story?'

The soldier's mouth opened in amazement and wonder. *But how,* he thought, *how?*

'Take the cards, boy.'

This made the soldier smile, for he was most definitely not a boy. But to the old man in front of him, he guessed he was. The soldier did as he was told, taking and placing the cards into his top, breast pocket for safe keeping. 'Thank you,' he said humbly.

'And take this.' The beggar reached under his chair with many creaks and many groans. He produced an old hessian sack, like the ones commonly used for spuds. The beggar held it out towards the soldier. 'Here you go.'

The soldier, not wishing to offend once again, took the sack, puzzling over the meaning of this gift. 'Erm, thank you,' came the soldier's reply in quizzical tone. 'I'm sure this sack will be handy for putting, erm, stuff in.'

'Don't be daft, boy,' came the scornful response from the beggar. 'This is no ordinary sack. This is a magic sack! You open this sack up and command any bird or beast into it and they will go. They will not be able to help themselves.'

The soldier did wonder on this. If this was true, why did this old boy look so underfed? Surely, he could have just caught himself a meal. 'Ok, yes, of course, how silly of me,' said the soldier. 'I look forward to trying this one out. Thank you.' And with that he said 'thank you' once more, and 'goodbye', and began, for the third time that day, along the long and winding road to who-knows-where.

Like a carthorse following a well-worn daily delivery route, the soldier's feet carried him down the road. Hunger and weariness became his companions, and he longed for the gentle embrace of a bed, down pillows and soft, woven blankets. The sun had not yet set, however, for it was summer and the days were long. He came at length to a large lake, upon which the sunlight danced over the ripples from the pleasant breeze. Stopping for a while to take in the tranquil beauty of the wooded shorelines and the rolling hills beyond in the late-afternoon/early-evening sun, the soldier noticed something on the water. There were three geese, minding their own business, going about their day, happy as the coot that sat on her nest nearby. The soldier's gaze flashed to the sack on his right shoulder, then back to the geese. *Surely not,* he thought, *but, worth a try?*

Opening the bag wide, the soldier, with hope and scepticism of equal measure in his voice, commanded the geese, 'Geese, Geese, I say, get in my sack!'

The order bounced over the water and into the geese's ears. Finding themselves compelled by a force stronger than their own will, the geese, in unison, turned and swam towards the shore where the soldier sat, sack waiting. In astonishment, the soldier watched one, two, three geese pile into the sack. The sack seemed at once to be full, but it seemed impossible for all three plump birds to fit in this small hessian bag. But alas, they did, and there they stayed, only the occasional muffled honk and ruffle of feathers giving their presence away.

The soldier's iron feet carried him once more down the road. As dusk hit, and the mellow mists rose from the valleys in the sun's final red light, the soldier came to the edge of a large town. Not having either the strength in body or fortitude of mind to explore this ancient-looking hub of civilisation, he beheld a truly wondrous sight: an inn! Behind its doors lay warmth, comfort, and friendship; the soldier knew this. Dragging his carcass through the door, the soldier fell upon a stool at the bar and surveyed the scene. A typical inn in a typical town. The same old collection of regulars nursing pints of beer, a log fire burning bright, even now in the height of summer, and a large, bearded, jolly fellow polishing a glass behind the bar.

'What can I get you, my good sir?'

'Sir?' remarked the soldier. 'That is a pleasantry I have never yet been given, but it is appreciated.'

The landlord spoke again. 'It looks, if you would forgive my forthrightness, like you are very weary, and that you have come many miles by many roads and are in need of some food, drink, and rest, sir.' Landlords and barmen have a knack when it comes to reading people, and this landlord had read the soldier like an open large-print book.

'Aye, that I have. I am on my way home after serving my time in the army, but, alas, kind sir, I have no idea where that may be, and,' the soldier looked down at his empty pockets, 'I have nothing to pay for lodgings and food…'

But then the soldier remembered the sack. He put it on the bar and said,

'In this sack are three live geese. If you were to cook one up for my supper, give me beer and lodgings for a few nights, would the remaining two birds do as payment?'

'Well, yes!' cried the jolly landlord. 'Yes indeed! I love a nice bird and just one goose, cooked and dressed, will fetch a pretty penny from a hungry party just off the road looking to fill their bellies. I doubt you could manage a whole one to yourself,' he exclaimed, 'but, you look hungry enough to try, I dare say. So, it is agreed.' He held out his hand. 'Food, being one of the geese, cooked and prepared, drink, and lodgings for several days, in return for two geese.'

Hands were shaken, and a deal was done.

'But be sure I get that old hessian sack back, mind,' added the soldier, 'for that old thing is very dear to me.'

'What? This old thing?' The landlord looked quizzically at the full sack, now in his hand. 'Well, each to their own I say. You shall have it back, that you will.' He smiled, turned on his heels and headed to the kitchen to dispatch of one of the birds, pluck and dress it, and get to roasting it.

It was near midnight before the bird had been cooked and the soldier was several sheets to the wind by then. The ale was fine and flowing, the company was fun and tuneful and, with the aid of the soldiers newly acquired ruby whistle, the inn was in fine spirits. The goose was presented to the soldier, roasted in cloves and honey, with vegetables to suit. A finer sight the soldier, and the company in the pub, had not seen in their lives. Without standing on ceremony, for his belly was shouting at him, the soldier forewent the eating irons laid on the table, using instead his bare hands. He devoured the succulent meat, sucked the bones, and drank the grease, until there was nothing but the bare carcass left. Not even the rats could find any pickings on it the next day when it was disposed of.

With a stomach fuller than he could remember, both of bird and beer, in the early hours of the next morning, the soldier climbed the old, crooked, wooden stairs to his lodging on hands and knees. His head hit the soft pillow, his eyes closed, and he was gone to the world. A dreamless sleep, such as the sleep of ages, washed over him, resting his body and mind. Never in his adult life had he slept so deeply and so contentedly than then.

The soldier awoke three days later. His eyelids crept open and the room around him came into view. Despite the volume he drank before he went to bed, he had slept through the hangover and now felt as fresh as summer daisies. He sat up, stretched and yawned. He could not remember when he had felt this refreshed and revitalised.

The sun shone through the window of his modest lodgings, comprising nothing more than the bed he sat upon, a simple chair and table in front of the window, and a wardrobe in the corner. That was fine by him. To the soldier, this was luxury. His newly revitalised legs lifted him up and his feet carried his curiosity to the window. There lay the town, stretching out before him. The inn was on top of a hill that looked over the tiled roofs down to the market square, with its many coloured canvases covering stalls selling all manner of food and wares. Beyond this, the soldier's eyes were drawn upwards. The land rose once more, mirroring the rise the inn sat upon. Perched like a topper on a cake was a building of wonder. Massive it was, and of the finest craftsmanship. The stonework for the walls comprised many coloured bricks creating arches and triangles, splitting off into many different turrets. Atop each turret sat a brightly coloured onion dome, no two the same in colour or design. One was azure and ivory; the next twisted upwards with emerald and mustard. The effect was both bizarre and joyful and made the soldier smile. He then noticed the windows. Even from this distance, he could tell they had been smashed. Then, looking harder, he realised the vast palace was empty and void of life.

The door creaked open and the landlord entered with a tray in his hands. Upon it was an array of cooked meats and pastries – a breakfast of kings. 'I thought I heard you up and about at last. I've brought you some breakfast. You must be famished after all this time.'

The soldier looked confused. 'All this time?'

'You've been asleep for three days, good sir. If it wasn't for your snoring, I'd have thought you dead!' And with this the landlord laughed his belly laugh.

'Three days,' mused the soldier. 'I must have needed it. Thank you,' he said, now looking at the landlord after snapping out of a daze, 'for the breakfast and the lodgings.'

'Not a problem,' he replied. 'I've sold both of those wonderful geese already and made a fine profit, so I have no problem with you staying a bit longer if you need. Oh!' the landlord reached inside his waistcoat. 'You wanted this back, I seem to remember.'

In his hand, the landlord held that old, battered, hessian sack. The soldier took it from him and smiled.

'Many thanks,' said the soldier, 'for this and for your kindness. It is just what an old soldier, down on his luck, needed. Now, tell me my good man, if you would, what that marvellous building over yonder is, and why all the windows are smashed?' His left hand pointed to the palace outside the window whilst his right hand grabbed a sausage and brought it to his waiting mouth.

'That? That's the tsar's summer palace?' said the landlord, wandering over to the window himself. 'The tsar used to come here every summer with all his retinue and hold balls week after week. Everyone was invited and everyone was involved.' The landlord gestured towards the palace, sausage in hand, a dreamy look of longing in his eyes.

The soldier looked puzzled and asked, 'Then, why is it empty and in such a state of ruin?'

The landlord's face dropped, and his head hung low. 'The devils came.' He sighed. 'The devils came one night, cleared the place out and partied all hours, playing cards, drinking, fighting…' The landlord's voice tailed off.

'Someone should do something about them devilish devils then!' replied the soldier.

'An army tried.' The landlord roused for the briefest of moments, 'but come the morning, there was nothing left of them, bar shadows and whispers.' His voice, once more faded into the morning sunlight, his mind lost in the sadness of those memories. 'That was the beginning of the end for this town. It's been going downhill ever since. The tsar has not dared to return, and many people have left for fear of the devils spreading out of the palace and into the town.'

Without the landlord noticing, the soldier had put on his boots and coat, picked up his cards, slung his sack over his shoulder and was heading to the door. Taking a bite out of the banger he'd taken from the breakfast platter, he remarked to the landlord as he left the room, heading for the stairs, 'I shall have to take a closer look then. This is far to interesting a story to pass up. Besides, it might be lucky. Who knows?' The soldier had that old storyteller's story ringing in his ears.

'Madness!' The landlord call after him, 'Folly! You go up there and you shan't be coming back, that's for sure. It was a pleasure meeting you, if only for a short time.' The landlord's words drifted after the soldier as he trotted down the wooden stairs, out the door and along the winding streets of the town, towards the old summer palace. The soldier knew not what he'd find, and cared not. He had nothing to live for and nothing to die for, so he was the perfect man to take a look at what was going on and to see what he could do.

The soldier took his time, strolling through the town, admiring the architecture, talking to the shopkeepers, the locals, and anyone who would spare him the time. Conversation of anything other than war had been sparce in his adult years, and it was a delight to now talk of simple things such as the weather and the coming good harvest. By the time he had made a town of new friends, sampled the wares the good folk had offered him, and filled his belly using nothing more than kind words and a genuine interest in people and their lives, the shadows were getting long and evening was drawing in. He approached the abandoned summer palace that looked even more marvellous close up, and even more dilapidated still. The soldier walked through the giant, wooden doors at the front, now hanging off their hinges like a drunkard hanging off a bar. He entered the large hallway with a once grand chandelier, now smashed in pieces upon the floor, stripped of all its precious stones. He paced slowly, into the great hall. This was where the grand balls were once held. It had borne witness to many fine dresses, to smooth gentlemen wooing pretty young women, to the finest musicians playing the finest music, and to the most delectable of foods from around the world, served for the party guests. Now, however, with the darkness growing out of every corner, all that was left was a long, wooden table, surrounded by chairs and stools, covered in a thick layer of dust and a handful of candlesticks.

The soldier took a seat, lit a candle and waited. As the gloom took hold of all but his pocket of candlelight, a grandfather clock somewhere down the many halls, kept wound by who-knows-who, echoed the strike of 9 p.m. The soldier pursed his lips together and began to whistle his ruby whistle to pass away the time.

10 p.m., the bells rang out, and nothing but the whistle sounded in those long-since deserted rooms.

11 p.m., and still only the bells and the whistle.

12 a.m., midnight. The witching hour. The bells struck each hour until the last stroke of midnight rang clear and loud through the palace. A sudden breeze, as if caused by a flutter of bat wings, blew out the candle. The soldier sat for a moment in the pitch black. No light, no shapes, nothing. But the soldier could feel them. A thousand eyes, menacing, piercing into his soul, slicing through the darkness. He could feel the movement of the air as a thousand

mouths breathed in the cool air and let go of the warmth within. Keeping his nerve, the soldier picked up the box of matches he had found on the table earlier and used to light the candle. He removed a match and struck it upon the side of the box.

'HISSSSSSS,' came the noise from all around. The light sparked from the match and onto the candle, which lit at once. It hit a thousand small, leathery red faces, which all recoiled in the sudden brightness.

'Oh, hello,' said the soldier, trying hard to steady his voice and stay calm. He shook the match out and placed it on the table, then looked around.

'HELLO?!' came the response from the creature nearest to him. 'He said, "Hello!"'

At this, the myriad of crimson critters burst into laughter. Their whole bodies shook with hysterics, shaking from their small horns upon their head, down through their bat-like wings, and to the tips of their cloven feet. The laughter was loud and raucous. The soldier simply ignored it.

'Hello,' the soldier repeated, cool as he could be. The laughter died down and the demonic yellow eyes of the creatures stared into him.

'Whose company do we have the pleasure of tonight? Pardon our manners. We haven't had guests in such a long time.' The largest, and, the soldier assumed, the leader, of the troop, spoke, trying to redeem himself and his fellow devils in the eyes of their new-found guest.

'Of course,' replied the soldier. 'You have my pardon.'

At this the devils sneered.

The soldier continued, 'I am just a poor old soldier, returning home from war. I hear you like playing cards and wondered if you'd like a game. If, of course, you have anything to wager?'

The little demons roared with delight.

'Oh yes,' said their leader. 'Yes, we love a game of cards. We play all night. Oh, yes, yes, we have something to play with...' and at this he motioned to the rest of the devils.

From trapdoors within the floor – once used to raise orchestras and performers out into the awaiting party goers to *oohs* and *ahhs* – came barrels and barrels, rolled by many devils.

'We have forty barrels of gold, which we have amassed over many years. Good enough?' He grinned a sharp, toothy grin full of malice and scorn towards the soldier.

'That'll do, I suppose,' came the soldier's response, cool, calm, and collected (on the surface).

'And what do you have, hey?' asked the devils. 'What do you have to wager?'

The soldier thought for a moment. He had nothing; only the clothes on his back and his precious sack, which he was not willing to give up. Besides, the devils would see no value in it anyway.

With no answer forthcoming, the devils began to list the things they personally wanted from the soldier:

'I want his ruby whistle. Yes, I heard him whistling that beauty, and that will make a fine prize!' said a smaller devil near the back.

'I want his teeth! I collect teeth.' With that, a scrawny, battered, deep burgundy devil pushed forward, showing off his necklace of human teeth around his neck.

'His soul...' came the deep, foreboding voice of the leader. 'I want his soul, to take back to the fires of Hell. I will enjoy tormenting your soul for eternity, soldier!'

Smiling still, and giving off an air of complete calm, the soldier replied, 'That seems fair.' With this, the devils rubbed their hands together, chattered with each other, and smiled. 'But...'

The devils' faces froze with this one word.

'But what?'

'But we play with my cards.' With that, the soldier pulled out the battered old pack he had been given by the beggar, what now seemed like a lifetime ago.

The terms of the game were set, the winnings agreed, and the cards were dealt by the soldier.

The first hand was played and the soldier won.

The second hand was played, and the soldier won.

The soldier won, and won, and won!

The devils cheated to high heaven and low hell, but to no avail. They tried every trick in the book but still had no luck. Of course, they couldn't call the soldier out for cheating, for they were doing it just as much, but far less successfully. Of course, the soldier was not cheating. It never crossed his mind to double deal, deal from the bottom of the pack, or hide cards up his sleeve. There was no need. He just kept on winning. He had seized his luck when he had the chance, and now he was reaping the rewards.

The devils fumed and fumed, as only devils can. Smoke rose out of their ears as the barrels of gold moved from their side of the table to the soldier's. Until, come the first rays of dawn, as the shadows of the old palace were being chased away by the golden hope of a new dawn, forty barrels of gold sat behind the soldier.

He gathered the cards up, put them in his breast pocket, and thanked the devils. 'Well gents, I think we shall call it a night, and I thank you very much for a very entertaining evening. Good morning.'

'No, we shall not call it a night!' screamed the leader of the devils, full of hatred and anger. 'We shall call this a breakfast, and you're the main course!' He was poised to pounce, ready to rip this worthless little man limb from limb.

'Before you do,' the soldier raised a hand, causing the devils to stop in sheer disbelief, 'tell me this. What do you call this?' The soldier held aloft the hessian sack, old, brown, and tatty in the morning light.

'A sack,' came the response from a thousand voices.

'Yes, just a sack, why?'

Their intrigue outweighed their rage for the briefest of moments.

'Well,' cried the soldier, opening the sack up wide, 'if this is just a sack, then by the grace of God, get in it!'

And with that command, the devils streamed into the old bag, one after another. Wings flapped furiously, claws clutched and scratched the table, but nothing could be done to stop each and every devil's fate. Into the sack they went, one by one, until they were all crammed inside. Impossible it seemed, to both the devils and the soldier, for a thousand devils to fit in such a small sack. But they were there, all together, and closer than they'd ever been before. Faces met parts of other devils that they had never dreamt of getting near.

The screams and pleas from the sack were loud and many. Shouts of, 'Let me out!' and 'Get that thing out my face!' came, alongside pleas of, 'We will do anything, ANYTHING!'

The soldier, having tied the sack up tight, took it outside into a once-beautiful but now overgrown courtyard where, in the first warming rays of morning sunshine, he swung the sack around his head, tossing it skywards and letting it fall with a thud on the floor. The devilish cries increased in volume and pitch, always pleading, always shouting for a stop to the torture – until, much to the creatures' delight, the sack was stationary. However, then came the sudden weight of the soldier, pressing down upon them as he sat on the bag. Slowly and carefully, he opened the sack to allow just the head of the leader to poke out.

'Please,' begged the devil, 'let us out! We will do anything!'

'Yes, anything!' came a chorus in reply.

'Well,' the soldier said, 'you are to leave this place, and my barrels of gold, and never come back.'

'Oh yes, of course,' grovelled the devil. 'Anything you say, Sire.'

'And make sure you clean the place up as you go,' the soldier added.

'Anything, of course, we will do anything, just please let us go!' The words were desperate in the devil's mouth. 'It stinks in here, even worse than the sulphurous fires of our home! We promise to tidy up and leave this place for good! On all that is evil and unholy, we promise!'

This was good enough for the soldier and so, he opened the bag fully and let the wretched creatures pour out into the golden rays of sunlight – all but the last one. He was skinny and scrawny, and the soldier caught hold of him by his left hoof.

'Not so fast little one. I'll be needing you, I'm sure,' said the soldier.

'Needing me?' came a small, scared voice from the young devil; the same voice that had requested the soldier's whistle if he lost at cards. 'Needing me for what, Sire?'

The soldier thought a thought, thinked a think and thunked a thunk, and then said, 'I don't know yet but, a wise old storyteller taught me the importance of seizing my luck when I get the chance. And, well, you are my chance. Just be there for me whenever I call. That is all I ask.'

The devil whimpered and squeaked. 'Anything, Sire! Yes, anything you say. I am forever at your service.'

And with an acknowledgement of this, the soldier gave the devil a shake by his cloven foot, which, to the soldier's surprise, popped off. 'Now, run along, and I shall keep this as a reminder to us both of your servitude to me.'

Well, wouldn't you know it, the devils were as good as their word, making good the palace in a matter of hours, restoring it back to its former glory. Then they were gone, as swiftly as they had arrived. The soldier then took up residence in the palace, sending word to the tsar of his deeds and inviting him to return to reclaim his long-lost palace.

Upon his return, the kindly old tsar gave the soldier many thanks for his service to the country, and for evicting the pesky devils. As a reward, the palace was left under the soldier's care, a home for him throughout the year. The tsar and his wife returned, summer after summer, and with them the balls and feasting returned. The town began to thrive once more, and the soldier and his exploits became legendary. The soldier himself fell in love, married and settled down. Before long a baby was born: a boy, who brought much joy and love to the soldier, his wife, and the palace.

However, this is no book of happy endings, as you know, so our story does not finish there. Oh no, this story is far from over. Fate had more in store for the soldier, you see.

One day, when the soldier's boy was around the age of 8, he became ill. The quacks and apothecaries were sent for. The finest physicians in all the land came to see if they could help the famous soldier's boy. But, alas, the boy's room filled with shaking beards and dour looks, before being replaced by a man in black measuring for a coffin for when the time would eventually come.

One morning, a morning bright and fine – much like that morning after the fateful night with the devils that seemed like a lifetime ago – the soldier and his wife stood in their son's room, holding each other tightly, bell-bottomed tears rolling heavy down their cheeks. Then the soldier's eyes fell upon the hoof of that devil of his. He'd had it mounted on a wooden plinth, and a strange black flower had grown from the ankle. The soldier's son had been so fascinated by it that his father had put it on his windowsill. Now it made the soldier harken back to that most gloriously famous of nights, and to that little devil he co-opted into his service.

'This illness of our boy,' came the words, creaking from the soldier's mouth into the ears of his beloved. 'It's the Devil's work for sure… and speaking of devils, where is that devil of mine?'

The soldier's eyes fell upon the cloven foot mounted on the plinth in the boy's window. All of a sudden, there was a puff of smoke and there, in the middle of the room, appeared the scrawny runt of a devil he had made a bargain with all those years ago – minus a foot, of course.

'Where did you spring from?' asked the soldier.

'Sire,' the devil bowed down low, 'forgive but, I did not spring – more like hopped, for you still have my foot.' And with that, a razor-sharp toothy grin came across the devil's face as he bowed once more to the ground.

'Of course, forgive me for my ignorance.' The soldier lifted the devil's head up and motioned towards his unwell son, lying on his deathbed. 'Tell me, is my son truly doomed to die? Is there nothing we – or you – can do for him?' The soldier had a look of hope and desperation etched upon his face.

The devil shifted on his stump and remaining good foot, hopping over to the child. He turned to the soldier to deliver his verdict. 'There is nothing on this Earth that can bring him back from the precipice on which he now stands, Sire.'

The soldier's face fell from hope to the deepest depths of despair. This little red fellow was his last roll of the dice. In that briefest of moments, he realised he would have to face the rest of his life without the one thing he loved most above all else; the best part of him; his future; his legacy to this world. His son meant more to him than any of his deeds at war or those after, even driving the devils from the castle. The soldier's son was his redemption. Through him, the soldier could look to amend the evils of war, and focus on the life he had brought to this world, rather than the death he had caused. For too long in his life, Death had been his bedfellow: his ever-present companion, the one constant, always by his side, taking those who were in the soldier's way and those by his side without care or consideration. The soldier had had enough of Death and his ways. But now, Death was knocking at the door of his son, and the soldier wanted no more part in Death's game. His time of keeping Death busy had gone, he now wanted to drive Death away. But it seemed to the soldier Death was not done with him yet.

'Oh, but not to worry,' came the cracked voice of the devil, looking up towards his master's face. 'I said nothing on this Earth.'

The soldier looked suddenly confused and the devil continued with a wry smile on his face.

'No, nothing on this Earth... but how about we try something not of this Earth?'

With this, the devil produced a crystal goblet out of thin air, which he filled with water from the jug beside the boy's bed.

'Now,' said the devil, handing the half-filled goblet to the soldier, 'look through this vessel at your boy and his bed and tell me what you see.'

The soldier, trembling with anticipation, raised the crystal goblet to his face. The sun, shining through the window, caught the etched glass and fractured into rainbows, sparkling and glinting in the soldier's hand. He peered through the goblet. Above the waterline he saw nothing unusual, but, below the water line – there, he saw it.

'I see something,' said the soldier, with a sharp intake of breath.

'What do you see?' prompted the devil, as the soldier stood there in awe, wonder, and fear.

'I see…' The soldier's brain cells worked overtime to decipher what his eyes were showing him. He began to speak, slower now, describing the scene in front of him, reversed through the refraction of the water. 'I see a figure. They are quite small and cloaked in black from head to toe. Their hands are resting on the bed, but those hands…' Again, the cogs in the soldier's brain ground round and round, processing the scene. 'They are not normal hands, for they have no skin or flesh. They are nothing but bone, bleached white like a carcass left in the sun.' The soldier's gaze rose to the head of this figure and he continued. 'Their face. Their face is… well, from what I can see under the-hood, it seems as white as their fingers. No skin. Yes, no skin on the face either.'

'That's Death,' said the devil. 'I believe you know him well, do you not, soldier? But I do not believe you have ever seen him face-to-face?'

The soldier gasped. 'This figure, he has been ever present through my life. He has taken everything I ever had, every friend I made, until now.' The soldier became angry at this thought. 'Not now, no!' cried the soldier in pain and anguish. 'Not my son! Have I not given you enough, with the souls I sent your way? Am I to be forever your harbinger, foreshadowing your arrival?' The soldier's free hand was now in a tight ball, his teeth gritted.

The cloaked figure moved not.

'Where is Death, Sire?' asked the devil.

The devil's voice snapped the soldier out of his fixation. 'Erm, he is at my boy's feet.'

The devil smiled his toothy grin and spoke in reply. 'That is good, then!'

'Good!' the soldier snapped at the devil. 'Death is sat by my boy's bed. I am to lose him, how is that good?' Anger and confusion darted across the soldier's face.

'If Death sits at the foot of the bed,' the devil explained, 'then we can help him. It's when Death sits at the head of the bed that we are powerless, and Death has decided on his next victim.' The devil now motioned to the soldier. 'Now, simply use your fingers to splash some of that water from the goblet onto your son, and Death will leave him and all will be well.'

Full of scepticism and hope now, the soldier did as he was instructed. And, as the devil promised, Death turned and walked away from the bed, before the boy opened his eyes and sat up in bed, feeling a lot better.

'A miracle! Huzzah!' cried the soldier, dropping to the bed to embrace his son. He turned, then, to the devil. The words of the story the storyteller told him many years ago ran through his mind, and said to the devil, 'Thank you, oh thank you, kind devil. You have done the kindest of things. If you leave me with that fantastic goblet, I will release you from my service and –' the soldier smiled and pointed to the window, '– I will give you back your foot.'

The devil's face nearly cracked open with the size of the smile that erupted on his face. No one had ever showed him kindness like this. 'Why, thank you, Sire! Thank you very much! I happily accept.' And with this, he left the soldier with the goblet, picked up the plinth-mounted foot, and vanished in a puff of smoke in the same way he had arrived, leaving a faint smell of sulphur in the air.

This was the soldier's chance to finally make amends for the death he had brought to the world, by saving those he could with this gift from the fires of Hell. He could not rid the world of Death completely, he thought, but he would chase Death away whenever he could. So, he set himself up as a miracle worker, travelling to lands far and wide, healing the sick, bringing them back from the edge of death. Rich men, poor men, beggars, thieves, even cats and dogs. The soldier discriminated not, for it was his calling now in life, to chase Death from place to place.

When he was called upon, the soldier arrived, filled the goblet with water and peered through. If Death was at the foot of the bed, then a simple splish, splash, splosh, and the poor soul was freed from Death's clutches, and everyone cheered and showered the soldier with gifts and money – whatever they could afford. If Death sat at the head of the bed, then the soldier explained there was nothing more he could do and apologised profusely. This mattered not, as the family were always glad he had come and tried and paid him all the same. Through this, the soldier became a very rich man, both in coin and in heart. He knew he was doing good and bringing joy to the world. Life was good… until news came that soldier had been dreading to hear, when he was as far from his home as he had ever been. The tsar was on his deathbed.

The soldier rushed home as fast as he could, but this still took many days, despite money not being an issue. Even all the money in the world cannot make horses pull the carriages any faster.

When he arrived at the summer palace, he was whisked up to the grand master bedroom. The tsar lay on the huge bed, with the ornate, decorative posts rising from each corner to a canopy above, flanked on all sides by the finest of curtains containing the most delicate and intricate of designs. The bed sat in the middle of the most opulent room the soldier had ever seen. The bed was surrounded by the brightest and best medical minds in the country, all of whom had shook their heads and agreed it simply was the tsar's time.

The soldier quickly filled the goblet and looked through it. He scanned the foot of the bed, and his heart stopped, as Death was nowhere to be found. He turned the goblet to the head of the bed, his heart now filled with dread. Sure enough, as he'd expected, there was his old adversary, Death, perched at the tsar's head.

'I've come too late…' mumbled the soldier, lowering the goblet and his head.

'What?!' spat the tsar's wife, the word like a venomous dart aimed at the soldier. 'What do you mean, "You've come too late?"'

The soldier saw the searching expression on the tsar's wife, covering the rage just below the surface. 'I've… I've come too late.' The soldier stumbled over his words. The room began to spin, and the enormity of the situation dawned upon him.

'You have been galivanting around the world, saving beggars and thieves, cats and dogs, but now – now you can't even save your Tsar.' The words came thick and fast from the tsar's wife's mouth, bearing all the hatred she was feeling right now towards the soldier. 'He has been like a father to you, taking you in when you had nothing, giving you everything, and now you cannot save him because you have come too late! Why? Why?' The repetition of the simple one-word question stabbed deep into the heart of the soldier, and the tsar's wife continued. 'I'll tell you why! You were too busy looking after yourself!'

The soldier thought for a moment, considering these words. He had told himself this mission of his was to benefit the world, but had it all been a personal vendetta? Was it all driven by his own desire to make right the wrongs he had done during war? How many did he have to save before the blood in his ledger was wiped clean? Yes, he was doing good in the world and bringing much happiness, but at what cost? Well – there was the cost, right there in front of him. Besides his son and his wife, the tsar had been the most important person in his life. And now, because he was miles away saving someone he had never met, he was going to die.

Lost in his own thoughts, the soldier was brought back to the room by one barbed, vicious word spitting from the tsar's wife's lips: 'Well?'

The soldier made up his mind. He knew what he had to do. He raised the goblet once more and looked at the cloaked figure. 'Death, listen to me and please, grant my request.' A tear rolled down his cheek as the soldier spoke. 'Please, leave the tsar a little longer. If you are in need of a soul this day, then have mine, I beg of you!'

The soldier's wife turned and fell at her husband's feet, yelling and crying, pleading he change his mind. But the deed was done. Death looked up and stared through the soldier's very soul with the hollows that should have contained his eyeballs. The soldier shuddered as Death nodded his head once, turned and vanished. It was then a simple splash of water from the goblet and the tsar arose, as happy and healthy as he'd ever been.

Celebrations were held that very night, toasting the tsar's miraculous recovery. But the hero of the hour, the soldier, now lay upon his bed, his wife and child next to him, readying himself to draw his last breath.

The soldier then raised the goblet of water up to his eyes and looked at Death, who sat firmly at the head of the soldier's bed. 'Death,' the words came out laboured and cracked. 'Death, before you take me, I have a question for you.' And with that, from under the sheets, the soldier pulled out something brown, musty, and old. 'Tell me, Death, what is this I hold in my hand?'

Death surveyed the brown material. It was hessian, he knew that, and it had been shaped into…

'A SACK,' came a voice, 'JUST AN OLD SACK.' Death's voice seemed to not come from his mouth but simply appeared in the heads of the soldier and his family.

'Well,' said the soldier, chancing a smile for what he hoped was about to happen, 'if this is a sack, then, by the grace of God, get in it!'

The soldier opened the sack wide with his free hand and an invisible force flew into the sack. Placing the goblet down in a flash, the soldier, suddenly feeling a lot better, tied the sack up tightly. He then began bouncing on the bed with his wife and son, feeling as healthy as he ever had. 'I did it!' he cried. 'I caught Death in my sack! Death is a prisoner!'

That phrase, 'Death is a prisoner', resonated throughout the palace and beyond. As the soldier scaled the highest hill nearby, that phrase echoed through the streets of the town. Climbing the tallest tree and edging his way to the end of the longest branch, the soldier tied the sack to it, and the phrase began its travels, from mouth to ear, to the borders of the country and beyond, spreading like gossip (and nothing spreads faster!). The soldier then fell out of the tree as he had secured the last knot securing the sack, but there is nothing like Death being off-duty to cushion a fall. The soldier stood up and brushed himself down.

That phrase was now on the lips of a million people, in a thousand different languages:

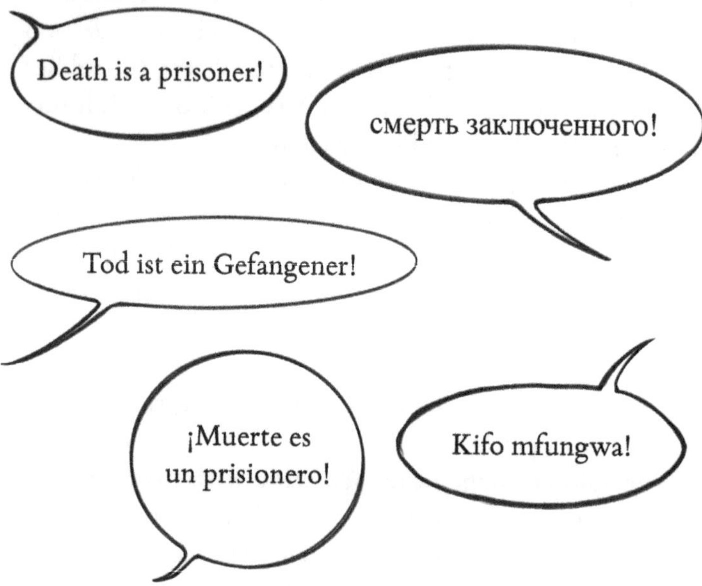

Death is a prisoner!
смерть заключенного!
Tod ist ein Gefangener!
¡Muerte es un prisionero!
Kifo mfungwa!

The soldier's latest deed was the talk of the world, and everyone celebrated. With no Death, nobody had to say goodbye to loved ones. There was no more mourning for those taken too soon or too cruelly. Without Death stalking the world, people believed they could now live a carefree life.

But, as the soldier returned to his home in the summer palace and the parties in his honour came to an end, the world started to look a bit different. A kind of different that got more and more worrying the longer you looked. Cattle and sheep would go to the butchers, only for the butchers' knives to simply slide over their necks. The butchers would sharpen their knives to a point so sharp they could split atoms, but to no avail. Armies threw themselves into battle at the start of the day, the air thick with cannon smoke and the sound of metal on metal. But come the end of the day, both sides stood there still, fully intact, all their soldiers still ready to fight – only minus some broken weapons and sliced off armour. Who had won? It was impossible to tell. Star-crossed lovers, forbidden to be together by their feuding parents, would throw themselves off lover's leap to be together forever in the afterlife... only to face a long walk back up and a bit of explaining when they got back home.

None of these things really impacted the soldier, until one day, several weeks later. He was standing by his bedroom window looking out across the palace gardens, which were still in full bloom, despite it being November. The gates to the gardens were always left open so the townspeople could enjoy this calm, tranquil place. But today, it wasn't the townspeople that the soldier saw strolling around, admiring the plants, but the elderly. So many of them – older than time itself, it seemed to the soldier – were standing, looking at the soldier's window, their eyes filled with hope and despair. It was in those old eyes, the eyes that had seen it all and were now tired of it, that the soldier saw his mistake. These people had all lived their lives. They had lived many years – some of them fuller than others – but all of them had *lived* just the same. It was their time to go: to leave this world, to slip into the gentle, quiet goodnight of death. They were waiting for Death's sweet release, but it just was not coming. They had nothing more to live for. They had made their peace with the world and now looked forward to the rest of wakeless sleep.

The soldier took pity on these poor old souls. He shed a tear, and knew what he had to do. With a nod towards them, he left the palace. He scaled the hill and climbed the tree as he had done a few weeks ago, and, with great care, brought down the old hessian sack. Sitting on the green grass, beneath the boughs of the tree bathed in autumn sunlight, the soldier opened the sack.

'Be free now Death,' he said. 'Be free, and forgive me for what I have done to you. Take me and continue with the work you have to do. You are as much a part of this world as birth, and I see that now. I was afraid of you; of losing more. You had taken so much from me and used me to take so many lives, I felt like a pawn in your game. But it is clear to me now, we are all pawns, simply playing our part, and this is as it should be. We play our parts before you come and take us away when we are done. Some of us have greater parts to play than others, some are only part of this game for a short, glorious time, but we are all fated to die eventually. Without death we cannot have rebirth – for we give way so that others can live, feel the world and all its emotions, sky-high love, the deepest laughter, the crippling sadness. I am not afraid, Death. Take me, please. I am ready.'

With that the soldier opened the sack wide and Death fled. He fled from that place and did not dare to turn back.

'Wait! Come back!' cried the soldier, but it was too late. Death was afraid of the soldier and his sack, of being removed from the world he loved so much and the work that brought him so much joy. Death, although he caused much sadness, gave great happiness to so many: those in pain, those who have lived their life and were ready to move on, and those who had simply had enough of this game of life. Yes, there were those who were not ready, but Death treated them kindly and showed them the way to the beyond with love, no matter which way they were heading – up or down. Death didn't look back, and he never dared come for the soldier again.

The soldier, having learnt the importance of Death in the world but still very much alive himself, returned back to the palace, and to his waiting family, whom he embraced. With Death now free, the world returned to normal. Star-crossed lovers were finally allowed to be together in the great beyond; battles were settled in the usual, bloody way, with all the waste of life that brought; and the animals felt the sharp blade of the butcher once more before gracing someone's table. But, above all else, those that had appeared in the palace gardens before the soldier's window – those who were waiting for Death and their eternal rest – welcomed him like an old friend. They gladly went with Death to their fate, be it good or bad.

The soldier lived his life as he had before, but without the miracle work. The goblet was stored away and forgotten about. Eventually, when the time was right, the tsar left this mortal coil, on the same night as his wife, which seemed fitting and just. The soldier smiled to himself, feeling this was a conscious decision on Death's part, after all that had happened. The soldier then had the heartache of watching his beloved wife fade away before she finally fell into that deep, dreamless sleep one cold winter's night in his arms. The soldier cried great, heavy tears, but accepted what had happened. But the soldier went on living. His beard grew ever longer and ever whiter, and he became as old and frail as the beggars he had seen all those many years ago on the roadside. He watched as everyone he had known and loved grew old, too. But then, unlike for him, Death came for them.

The worst was yet to come, though. No father should ever have to bury their own child, even if they have lived a long and full life. Knowing his son had lived well was the only ray of light in an otherwise truly dismal day for the soldier. Saying goodbye to his son was the final straw, and the soldier's back was well and truly broken. No longer could he remain there, in the palace where he had lost everything and everyone he had ever loved. So, taking just the essentials, his lucky playing cards, and, of course, the hessian sack, he set off to walk the world, hoping to find a way down.

Down he walked, down and down for many years, until he felt it getting hotter, and the smell of rotten eggs filled his nostrils. And there they were in all their glory. The heavy, iron gates of Hell, glowing with the heat from within. The soldier lifted his heavy hand and knocked three times.

To his surprise, it wasn't the main gate that opened but a smaller one, high up and to his left, out of which came a familiar-looking leathery red face. 'Yes, can I help?'

'Oh, yes,' replied the soldier, relieved the devil did not now recognise the withered old man at his front door.

'Well,' prompted the devil, 'get on with it you old fool, we haven't got all day. Why are you here?'

'I am a poor old soul who seems to have been missed by your good friend Death. I am ready to die, and realise I will not get into Heaven with the sins in my ledger, so I am here now to surrender my soul to the fires of Hell.'

Well, this was very unusual, thought the devil. This had never happened. Normally souls were dragged in kicking and screaming. They didn't walk in voluntarily. *This will be fun,* he thought, *trying to break this one*. But it was at this time, when the devil was looking the old man up and down, trying to think of the best ways to torture him, that his eyes fell upon a swath of hessian over the man's left shoulder. 'Wait, what's that?' asked the devil, pointing to the soldier's shoulder.

'This?' replied the soldier. 'Oh, this is nothing, just an old sack of mine that has seen me right throughout the years.'

With that, the devil's head vanished back into the little door, and it slammed shut.

'Wait, where are you going? Are you not going to let me in?' The soldier's voice strained with desperation.

'It's that bloody sack, I knew it! We know who you are, and we remember what you did to us.' The voice echoed from behind the iron door, accompanied by a chorus of grating voices crying out in agreement. 'Get that bloody thing away from here!'

The soldier was defiant. He had come too far to give up now. 'Fine,' he declared, the seed of an idea taking root in his mind and blooming in a matter of seconds. He may have been old, but his brain was still as sharp as his old sword. 'If you won't let me in, then you will give me two hundred souls that have served their time in the fires of Hell and are waiting to go to Heaven, so I may bargain my way in there.' He knew this was desperate, but it was worth a shot.

There was much discussion and muttering from a thousand harsh voices behind the doors before him. The small upper door creaked open, and a leathery face peered out.

'One hundred and fifty!' came the haggling response.

'Two hundred,' the soldier replied, holding fast. 'You do remember what this thing does, don't you?' The soldier raised the sack aloft, and the devil coward back into the doorway.

'Fine, two hundred!' shrieked the devil. 'Take 'em and be gone!' Braving a look over the door's threshold, the devil said his parting shot, 'Have 'em, for what good they'll do you! And don't shake that thing at me!'

The order fell upon the soldier's broad shoulders and ran off like water from a duck's back. He once more flailed the sack in the general direction of the devil, who yelped and disappeared, slamming the door behind him.

The soldier watched as the larger doors rumbled open and two hundred figures tramped out, dressed in rags, their heads hung low, their steps weary and pained. As the last one left, and the doors began to close, a battered old scroll came hurtling out of the crack, striking the soldier on the back. He turned and picked it up, unrolling it. A devil's voice came from behind the door.

'There you go, a map to Heaven. And don't say I never give you anything.'

The soldier recognised this voice. It was the devil he had held in his servitude. 'Why, thank you, old friend.'

'Don't say that too loud,' replied the voice. 'The others might hear, and I'd be mortified. Look, follow the map and keep going until you get the feeling you're standing on your head and you hear church music. Then you know you're there.' Subsequently, in a hushed voice, the devil said, 'Good luck, and thank you.'

Onward and upwards the soldier led the souls. Following the map, he crossed through the land of the living, which now looked so different and uninviting. He had but one thought on his mind: eternal rest. Upwards still they climbed, until the air was filled with the sound of organs and angelic choral voices and bright light. There, in front of them, stood a tall figure robed in the brightest of white, with a beard rivalling that of the soldier's in length. Before him stood a lectern of gold, and upon it, a book filled with names.

'Halt, who goes there?' St Peter's voice resonated through the soldier's body and beyond; deep, booming, forceful, but kind and caring.

'Alas,' the soldier said, bowing his head low in respect, 'I am the soldier who foolishly caught Death in my sack. I have been to the fires of Hell to rescue two hundred souls who have served their time and are now ready for the caring embrace of Heaven. I hope, for this good deed, that my previous sins may be erased, and I may be allowed to enter to be with my family once more.' The soldier looked upon St Peter with eyes wide and full of the hope of a hundred lifetimes. He had tried to live his life the best he could, to seize the luck that was out there waiting for him. But one mistake, one misstep, for the benefit of someone he loved, had cost him everything. This was the last roll of the dice, his final chance, and his heart stopped for the briefest of moments awaiting the response.

'The souls may enter,' boomed the voice of the gatekeeper, as he looked through his names in his book, 'but you may not.'

The soldier's heart stayed still and unbeating for the briefest of seconds, but then began its rhythm again. For if it were to stop, the soldier would get his wish and finally die – but that was not his fate, it seemed. He watched on as the pearly gates opened and the souls began to enter but, try as he might, his feet would not carry him past the threshold. He could not see what lay beyond – only white light and the feeling of love and kindness seeping out and overflowing down into the world.

He turned to see the last soul in the line come near and, as he did, his face brushed that old sack of his, still on his shoulder, as it had always been. Once more, that sharp old brain of his had an idea. He had thought this was it, but no, there was one more thing he could try.

'Here, friend,' the soldier said to that last poor soul, handing him the old hessian sack. 'Take this and, when you get over the threshold, open it and tell me to jump inside. Please,' he said, his face full of hope, 'remember that I saved you from the fires of Hell. This is your chance to save me.'

Well, the soldier watched in anticipation as the last of the souls, with the sack in his hand, stepped into paradise and vanished into the light. He stood, and he waited. He watched as the pearly gates closed, and he waited. He waited. He waited.

Heaven is said, by those that believe in such a place – whether they call it Heaven, Jannah, Nirvana, Valhalla, Zion, or anything else – to be a place of pure bliss. There, we are happy and content, never wanting, never fearful, and never thinking of our past life. We forget the rigours and tribulations that tested us through life, for we are at peace. And so it was for that soul with the sack in their hand. As they passed over into Elysium, he dropped the sack from his hand, forgetting the soldier, the fires of Hell, and all that had come before. For now they were happy and restful.

The soldier, after waiting for many hours and many days, turned his weary, heavy body around towards the world and began to trudge back, accepting his fate at long last. His fate was to forever live on this Earth. He would go on when all else faded. He would see empires rise and fall, kings and queens come and go, new technology advance the human race, leaving him further and further behind, while he endured. He was a legacy, a nugget of history, a keeper of the stories of those times gone by – not because he had heard them all but because he had been there and lived these stories. He had seen war and peace, saints and devils. He had seen it all and was still there to tell the tales.

And how do I know this, and how do I know his story, you may ask? Well, he told it to me. For he still wanders this world, even today; my friend the soldier. His beard now brushes the floor, and his skin has more wrinkles than the sand of the shoreline at low tide, but he keeps on keeping on. He's a good man who deserves better luck. But he whistles that ruby whistle of his, tells his stories, and gets a farthing from time to time to see him right. But, my friends, listen here. If you meet my old friend the soldier, after you have said hello from me, heard his stories, and marvelled at his whistle, say your goodbyes. Do not, DO NOT play him at cards!

THE SAILOR AND THE MERMAID

For the last story in my book, I have chosen another all-time favourite. I originally heard the wonderful Afro-Caribbean storyteller Jan Blake tell this story some years ago at the wonderful Festival at the Edge storytelling festival. Her set of stories followed black slaves from Africa to the Caribbean to America, all accompanied by the brilliant playing of a fiddle. Jan has such a warm, friendly way of storytelling, and the music was so wondrous she only managed to get to the Caribbean, and her second story, and it was this one that really stuck with me.

The main character within this story for Jan's version was Black. However, I have changed him to a white British man for my version. I strongly believe in 'write what you know' and, as a white male, I would feel somewhat hypocritical telling this story as it was told by Jan. Storytellers change stories all the time and so this was no different. Stories migrate to different cultures and the characters change, but the core of the story remains the same. Over my years of telling this, the character took on the name he has now, John, and the 'John Konaka' song was added, which works beautifully as an opener when told to a live audience. The other song, 'Drunken Sailor', with its changed lyrics, was also added as it seemed to fit and adds to the telling, giving it more depth and texture.

While writing this story, my curiosity was piqued regarding the origins of the name used in the famous sea shanty. This led me down a rabbit hole of research and a frantic cross-reference of dates to see if the Hawaiian origins in the story work with the timeline I have created. I can say it does, just about. The story describes John sailing with the famous pirate captain Calico Jack, when John is a lad, but Jack died in 1720. If we assume then that John sailed with Jack when John was a young teenager and Jack was nearing his hanging at the age of 37 (around 1719–20), that predates James Cook's official discovery of Hawaii by almost 60 years. However, it is almost certain that other western sailors and pirates had come across this volcanic island chain beforehand, so having John be there when he is older, around the age of 50, becomes very plausible and doesn't shatter the illusion too much. Although this is not a historic story and not based in fact, sprinkling it with believable truths and references helps make it more engaging.

As for John's early life in Robin Hood's Bay: this was inspired by a chance viewing of a BBC documentary series called Villages by the Sea. *I have been to this wonderful little port many times, but this programme opened my eyes to the smuggling past of the village and set my imagination soaring, resulting in the flashbacks you will read.*

For the mermaid, it was hard not to base her loosely upon the iconic Arial from Disney's The Little Mermaid, *although I try hard to give her a distinct character. Before mermaids were Disneyfied, they often took on a very menacing presence in folk tales. They were feared by sailors as they would warn them of dread and doom; or they were the sirens of Greek mythology who sang the ships to dash upon the rocks. I have therefore used this story to give a plausible explanation as to why we have the two conflicting views of these sea-dwelling creatures, and created a believable reason for them to turn against humans.*

A lot of research and time went into this story. Even my wife, my biggest critic, praises it as one of my best. I have asked her to write that praise down so I can frame it for the future, but she has sadly vetoed that.

Enjoy the story.

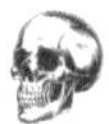

I thought I heard the old man say (hoo!)
(John, Kanaka-naka, too-rye-ay)
Today, today it's a holiday (hoo!)
(John, Kanaka-naka, too-rye-ay)
Too-rye-ay, oh! Too-rye-ay
John, Kanaka-naka, too-rye-ay
We're bound away at the break of day (hoo!)
(John, Kanaka-naka, too-rye-ay)
We're bound away for 'Frisco Bay (hoo!)
(John, Kanaka-naka, too-rye-ay)
Too-rye-ay, oh! Too-rye-ay
John, Kanaka-naka, too-rye-ay.

Nobody knew quite who John was. He lived on a Caribbean island, on his own, in a tumble-down old shack as aged and creaky as he. His days and evenings were spent sinking pint after pint of ale in the local tavern on the far side of the crystal-clear bay. Most of the drink made its way into his mouth, but some would often escape into his full, grey beard, staining it in streaks of yellow and brown. The bits of face that the patrons of the tavern could see were dark brown and wrinkled like a well-used leather coat. John's hands around the tankard had seen hard work. Those hands had pulled on many yards of rough rope, hauling and heaving great weights time and time again. A hard exterior mirrored a hard life lived.

People guessed he was an old sailor. His raspy voice often spoke in snippets of far-off lands and troubles upon the sea, but his stories remained vague, leading people to question whether they were his lived experiences or second-hand news gained from others during drinking sessions in various ports across the world. Occasionally, John would catch himself and stop short of dropping a meaty morsel for the listeners, leading some to believe he was not just any old sailor but a buccaneer, privateer or even a pirate. Never was a ship or captain's name mentioned, never a trade route shared. The listeners to John's stories had to fill in the gaps, and the gaps were many and large. But people loved it. John was the storyteller of the island. Without saying much at all, he could tell of tales from across the known world and beyond. The lack of detail only enhanced the mystery and left the listeners' minds open to build the details for themselves.

John had spoken in his few words of many things that were thought to be myth and legend. He casually dropped into conversation his near-miss with the Hafgufa, an island-sized beast from Nordic mythology. No details were forthcoming though; just a mention of its size and location, somewhere in the North Sea. Once, he stated he'd seen a ship dragged to Davy Jones's locker by the great Kraken itself. More details on that were given by John: details of the ginormous tentacles that wrapped around the middle of the craft, snapping it in two like it was made of nothing but matchsticks, then hauling it beneath the waves. But there was one creature from the deep which John often spoke of: mermaids. In his time on the ocean waves, those beauties of the deep were considered good omens. If you were blessed with good fortune you would see these creatures, half-fish, half-nymph-like woman, riding the bow wave in front of the ship like dolphins. John was blessed with seeing this spectacle many times during his years, and had fallen in love with the innocence and wonder of these creatures. Straddling the line between the land and the mysteries of the hidden kingdom in the deep, they held infinite intrigue for all sailors, and none more so than John. For it was his only regret in life that he had not managed to garner a kiss from these mythical wonders. His eyes would mist over, and he would taper off into quiet contemplation when the subject arose. *Just one kiss,* he would think to himself, *just one.*

John's days followed a regular pattern, which he liked. By midday he was in the tavern by the bay, drinking mostly alone, which he also liked. He would eat lunch, dinner and supper there, drinking until the late hours when the barman would roll him out and tell him to go home. He was never a bother to anyone, always had the coin to pay his dues, and left when asked. He was just very aloof, unless engaged in his tale telling. The people around him tried to guess at his past, but they had no idea of the things he had seen and done in his past life – acts so horrendous they would turn even the strongest of stomachs and make them feel like a landlubber on the wildest of oceans. But he had left that life behind and would revisit those times only during his sleep. The dreams were vivid and hard to take, and so he found drinking until he passed out the best way to keep them at bay. Once turned out of the tavern, he'd stagger around the bay and upward to the low-lying cliff on the far side on which his shack stood. It overlooked the bay, framed with palm trees, but he did not spend much time there. The ale was in the alehouse, not in his home.

When our story starts, the moon was big and bright and full over the bay, its silvery light reflecting off the smooth waters below. John had drunk more than his share that night after falling into a story of his time on the sea, while trying hard not to give too much away. This was hard and he required more beer to concentrate. Now, as the midnight hour passed, he was turfed out of the tavern and slowly, and clumsily, made his way home and to the embrace of his unmade bed. On the way, his sunken eyes fell upon a sight he had not seen in many a moon.

The tide was low that night and it had exposed a single, rounded rock that had been worn smooth by the ebbing and flowing of the tides over the years. Normally this rock was frequented by gulls and terns, their defecations washed clean away come the next high tide. But tonight a wholly different creature adorned the boulder before him. A young woman, looking no more than 20 years of age, fair in skin and hair, perched there before the drunkard's gaze. John watched in awe as she delicately combed her hair, her back to him as she stared out to sea. Within her slight, dainty right hand she held a comb, which she glided through her long, blonde hair that sat lank and damp upon her almost translucent skin. John's lecherous gaze followed the contours of her naked torso downwards to where her skin gave way to shimmering, shining scales, blue and green and all the colours in-between, in the light of the silent satellite above. The form then changed from a human body to a large fish tail, curled and wrapped around the rock. The delicate tail sat upon the water, rising and falling with the rippling waves.

The mermaid was blissfully ignorant of the lust and malice now rising through the old sailor's veins like sap in spring causing the buds to emerge. It was having a similar effect on John also. He felt drunken stirrings within his depths; stirrings in places he'd long forgotten about. But now, faced with this beauty, the object of his lust and desire for so much of his adult life, and having more alcohol in his veins than blood, he needed to act. He snuck as stealthily as a drunk man can into the shallows towards the object of his desire. He had all the grace and elegance of a fairy elephant.

Just one kiss, he thought. One kiss and he would be happy. *Of course,* he also thought, *if it turns into anything more I would not say no. How would it even work?* his thoughts continued. *She's half fish; the half where all the action happens. What does she have down there? Would it even work?*

The mind of this inebriated old sea dog wandered like a ship blown off course without a compass. He forgot about being stealthy just as he entered the water. A great splash he made as his toes caught on a submerged rock. He tumbled forward, lurching and holding out a hand toward the mermaid. Her head spun around to see the lecherous old man grasping at her. He was drenched from head to foot, his stained white beard drooping lank into the water, rising and falling with the waves. She saw the cavernous lines upon his ancient face and the look of yearning in his eyes. This old man wanted to take this young mermaid for his own, and she knew this was wrong.

Acting purely on instinct, much as a rat bolts when a light is turned on, the mermaid dived into the crystal-clear waters, making barely a splash, leaving only the slightest of ripples. She was an arrow darting into the water straight and true, a dive far surpassing even the greatest of high divers. John lunged forward, grasping at the air, but he wasn't even close. He fell, walrus-like, upon the stone where the mermaid had been but moments before.

He lay there processing the situation. His greed and desire had cost him the one thing he wanted more than anything in this world. If he had been slower, more considered, more courteous even, there surely would have been more of a chance. But, he knew, it was the mead and the rum sitting heavy in his belly – that made the world spin and rock, that settled him, giving him relief from the stillness of land – that had clouded his mind and judgement and let him be led by his loins rather than his head. His chance had gone. He took in a deep breath of the salty sea air and exhaled into the warm night.

As he lay there, gazing hazily into the shallow water beneath him, he noticed something. In amongst the pebbles and stones, the anemones and seaweed, something caught the moonlight, glinting back at him. He strained his eyes to see more clearly what it could be before plunging his arm into the water and taking hold of it. He lifted it out. It was only slightly bigger than his hand. He recognised the glistening white and rainbow colours that caught the light and made it dance and play. This was the inside of a large clam shell, a wondrous mother-of-pearl. He wondered at the precise carving of delicate teeth down one edge. Two or three teeth were missing, suggesting the shell was of some age, and John knew age meant value. This was a comb – the comb the mermaid had used to brush her hair. A real-life mermaid's comb! He had never seen one himself but he'd heard tell of such items being found by sailors – and the small fortunes they were sold for. He may have missed out on a mermaid's kiss, but in his hands was enough money to see him in mead and rum for the rest of his landlocked life.

Holding the treasure tight in his hand, he stumbled toward the shore. There is nothing like a late-night dip in the cold ocean and the discovery of something that will make your fortune to sober you up. Soaked to the skin, John hauled himself up the steady slope around the bay to that hovel he called home. It wasn't much to look at, but it was weather-tight and secure, and that was all that mattered to John. Once he had followed the gravel path up to his front door, he fumbled for his keys and found them still safe in his trouser pocket. Unlocking the door with a key the size of a baby's arm, he fell into the darkness beyond. Although sleep was beckoning him, he still had enough wits about him – or was it just habit – to turn on his heels, slide the key into its home, and lock the door. It was then just a short stumble across the relatively empty room – mostly devoid of furniture, save a chair in the corner – to the bed on the far side. Of course, the bed was unmade, the sheets having been thrown in a heap on the straw-filled mattress, but with his eyelids now betraying him, he cared not and soon fell into that heavy sleep that comes from too much liquor. But his hand stayed tight around the night's ill-gotten gain. It was not stealing, but the rule of finders-keepers – or so he told himself. It was his now, and he was going to profit from it.

The night drew on. It was that time of the night when the moon had gone to bed but the sun was still only beginning to think about coming up, and so the sky was as dark as it gets. A sound cut through this inky blackness, making its way through the door and windows of John's house and into his ears. He stirred, the sounds causing bizarre images to form in his unconscious mind before one of his eyes failed to resist the urge to open. The other soon followed suit and there he lay in complete darkness, awake but still. He continued to listen to that sound that crept up the hill towards the cabin, getting louder and louder. He then realised there were two distinct sounds. The first he recognised instantly. It was the sound of nails on fingers scraping through gravel and dirt, with the arms pulling something forward. The second took a minute for his brain to decipher and catch up. It was a wholly unexpected sound to hear in the dead of night there at the top of the cliffs overlooking the bay, and it sent chills down his spine and goosebumps raising on his neck. The sound was a slapping sound – a slapping sound he had heard many times before. This was the noise of the fish being slammed down upon the fishmonger's block in the port, before the fishmonger went to work gutting and paring the soon-to-be food item in front of him. That slap was clearly a fish's tail making contact with the ground, but this tail was far larger than anything John had seen at any fishmonger's. This was on par with a shark or a dolphin.

His ears strained and listened, heightened by the lack of light, hearing the two sounds – the scrape and slap – getting ever closer and closer. He had put two and wo together and figured out what was coming for him. It was the mermaid he had scared off with his advances. Or was this a relative? Maybe it was an elusive, scarcely seen merman, come to take what belonged to his daughter or lover by force. John's heart raced at these thoughts. He was too young to die, he tried to kid himself. In reality, he was living on borrowed time and he knew it – everyone knew it – but it helped his self-esteem to tell himself little lies.

His thoughts suddenly turned to something else as the noise was now outside his front door. Did he lock the door? He remembered coming in, but the rest was a blur. His habit was normally to lock the door but with everything that had happened, maybe he had forgotten this time. He lay frozen in place in the bed, hoping, wishing, praying he had locked the door. The handle began to turn slowly before rattling. The door held fast and John's heart slowed with relief. He had locked the door!

Then came a slow and considered knock at the door. The rat-a-tat-tat rang clearly and echoed around the empty room. This was pursued by a voice – young, sweet and innocent, childlike, almost, in its inflections. It was a female's voice, soft and frail, and it said this:

'Please Sir. Me comb, Sir. 'Ave ye got me comb, Sir?'

John clutched the comb tightly; he had been holding it tight throughout his slumber and was not about to let go of it now. Finders, keepers.

'Please, Sir,' came the pleading voice once more. 'Me comb, Sir. It were me Ma's comb and her Ma's before that. It means so much to me, Sir. Could I please 'ave it back?'

John felt the slightest prang of guilt hit him for the slightest of moments; a mere chink of remorse trying to escape from his stone-cold heart. But he did what he had always done, and buried it deep down low, never to be heard from again. He was hard and fast, like the rocks that stuck out of the sea that careless or unlucky ships were cast upon. He was a rock, an island devoid of emotion now, and this priceless gem was his. He held it tighter still.

The pleading had not worked. The poor mermaid had realised this, so she moved on to her next gambit. She began to sing. Her voice was high and clear; a voice that could herald in the dawning of a new day full of hope but also be a portent of doom. Both beautiful and terrifying all in one note.

What shall we do with a drunken sailor?
What shall we do with a drunken sailor?
What shall we do with a drunken sailor,
If he don't give me comb back?

Pull him down to Davy Jones's locker,
Pull him down to Davy Jones's locker,
Pull him down to Davy Jones's locker,
If he don't give me comb back.

The words were familiar but foreign all at the same time, and all directed, John knew, directly at him. As he listened, he found his legs swinging out of bed and he sat bolt upright. He fought his movements – with every sinew in his body he fought – but to no avail. The words, the haunting voice, compelled his body to move, now upright. He placed one foot after another, carrying his unwilling body across the room to the door, his face covered in a grimace. At the halfway point, John's every muscle straining to stop the march, the singing ceased without warning – as did John's body. He stood stock still in the gloom, not daring to move, his ears straining against the new silence for clues as to what might happen next. He then heard the mermaid outside turning, and the eerie sound of scraping and slapping slowly working its way down the path back to the sea.

When the noise had gone and all was safe, John returned to bed, still tightly clutching the mother-of-pearl trinket. As he lay in his bed, his eyes slowly closing, he resolved to take the comb to the marketplace first thing in the morning to get rid of it. He could not risk what might happen if the siren's song brought him all the way to the door the next night.

The swell was high – higher than he had ever known it. Giant white horses broke hard over the bow, sending sailors rolling down the deck like skittles in a bowling alley. John's first experience on a large sailing ship was certainly proving to be eventful. Just two days prior the main sail ripped in two during a freak storm off the east coast of Ireland. As the youngest, fittest, and most nimble, he was sent up the rigging to untie the lashings that held the sail firm on the cross-member of the main mast. His hands were numb by the time he reached the top. It was like trying to knit a cardigan with blocks of ice. Pretty soon, relief arrived in the form of a more experienced sailor, who swiftly untied the tattered sheet with a few skilful tugs on the ropes. John watched and learnt, he took in everything like a sponge, and he would know for next time. But the untying of ropes he had learnt a few days ago was no good now.

He was used to the familiar swaying of wood beneath his feet, floating upon the ocean. As a young boy he went out with his father in the small coble boat the family owned and made a simple living catching lobster, crab, cod, and other sought-after fish that they would gut and dry outside their house. These would sell for a tidy profit, being coveted across the world. The rocky sea floor off the coast of Robin Hood's Bay was ideal for this, as only these small coble boats could navigate the shallower waters. Larger ships had to dock down the coast at Whitby, which is where John had found himself a month prior. He was there to pick up supplies for the family's boat – new rope, hooks, and other various consumables – when he was whisked away by some strong-armed seafarers. They told him this would be the making of him and that they would see to it his family were informed and reassured all was well, but the look John saw in those chiselled, gritty men's eyes told a different story. John had always been a good judge of character. He had the instincts of a dog, his father would say in a kindly fashion, able to sense the true worth of a person.

Now, this rough sea was a million miles away from what he considered a big swell of around six feet back at home. These waves towered over the ship, blocking out the light from a misty sun. He held fast to a coil of rope secured to a cleat at the starboard side of the vessel. The last thing he remembered were the cries of fear from the crew as the colossal wave bore down upon them, and the sheer weight and force that hit him like a brick wall falling from the sky – and then, nothing.

John slowly opened his eyes. The golden sunlight crept like treacle through the tattered scraps of cloth he called his curtains and spread itself upon his bed. He lay there, fully clothed from last night, still damp and smelling of the sea. He stayed there a while, breathing in that wonderful smell; a smell that brought back so many memories, both good and bad. He had spent a lifetime smelling that salty scent and it had become the smell of home for him, far more than any dusty cabin, no matter how perfect the location.

Rolling out of bed, he hit the floor with a thud. Peeling off his damp clothes like layers of an over-ripe onion, he looked around for some dry ones. It mattered not if they were clean; he just needed to be dry. He had learnt the hard way that you always got into dry clothes as soon as you could. Nasty things happened to your skin when it stayed damp for too long, and he had the scars to prove it. Once dry and dressed, he rummaged in the bedsheets and found the comb. In the shafts of sunlight, he looked upon it once more. He had feared it had been a dream or hallucination brought on by the mead and rum, for his head was certainly telling him he had consumed a fair quantity. The treasure in his hand now confirmed his experience was real, which then jolted him into remembering what he must do. He could not risk another visit from that siren of the sea; risk opening that door; risk being shown Davy Jones's locker up close and personal by a vengeful sea creature. So, he vowed, to the market it must go to fetch a fine price for a fine piece.

On went the trusty old boots that had seen him halfway across the world and back, and his hand fell upon the large iron key that sat in the lock of the door. He thanked his lucky stars his wits held out enough last night for him to have turned this metal in that hole. With a heavy clunk and an aged creak, he opened the door. As he went to step out into the wide world he froze in awe and wonderment. Piled high upon his doorstep was a heap of treasure! He had heard tell of treasures like this from sunken ships, laying on the ocean floor, or buried on some remote island, only being located by a map with an X to mark the spot. But here in front of him lay gold, silver, diamonds, emeralds, and jewels of all kinds, cuts, and carats. The haul was around six feet in diameter and at least four foot in height: a mix of coins, decorative items, jewellery, and tableware, all covered in a shimmering residue of saltwater and the odd strands of kelp and other seaweeds. John took a moment to marvel at the wonder before him before picking his jaw up from the floor. His head then swivelled around like an owl's to see if anyone was looking, but the landscape was empty for many miles, until the tavern in the bay below. With haste, he gathered the treasure inside, piece by coin, cup by ring. He lifted one of the floorboards and stashed it away, out of sight – a trick he'd acquired in his youth.

The crown levied heavy taxes upon products arriving in Britain to pay for the wars with their neighbours in Europe. For a nation that ran on tea this was a problem, as it had become too expensive to be enjoyed by the common man. And so, there became an opportunity for those willing to exploit it. John's house in the bay sat above a stone culvert that directed the King's Beck, a small stream running off the desolate moorland above through the cleft in the cliffs into which the community was built. The beck ran out of an archway onto the beach below and was tall enough for a man to walk almost upright, and for at least two men to comfortably walk abreast for a fair distance before they'd have to go single file and stoop slightly. It was at around this part that John's family house happened to have a very handy trapdoor built into the floor of the kitchen. It was meant, John presumed, to originally be for the discarding of dirty water and scraps to be washed out to sea. It had now become a very useful entry point into the house.

John, being the smallest of five boys, often had the job of being lowered down the trapdoor. He had to make his way to the exit of the culvert and look for the small row boats that carried the contraband to shore. When he spied the short, sharp flash of light, the signal he'd been waiting for, he would return to the trapdoor to tell his parents so they could ready for the arrival of the smugglers. John had just a candle to light his way, and often the wind whipped up the culvert and blew out his light source, and he would have to feel his way along. He became good at seeing the shapes of things in the dark, his eyes adjusting quickly. He knew every rock and hole in that culvert.

The smuggled in tea, alcohol, and other sought-after goods, which were then packaged beneath the dried fish in the carts and wagons to be taken over the moors to larger towns such as Scarborough to be sold for a great profit. John's family were very wealthy but knew not to show it. To the eyes of anyone looking on, they were just a humble fishing family just getting by.

It was two of the smugglers, John guessed, that took him on that fateful day in Whitby. They knew his talents and that he could keep a secret and that he would be an asset.

John's head span. A lifetime he had spent in pursuit of riches and, although he was comfortable, he had never amassed the wealth he had craved. This was it, this was his chance, his luck that he'd been waiting to seize! For too long had life been seizing him, sweeping him up from one caper to the next, never knowing what was around the next corner, what ship he would be sailing on next, which side of the law he would be on. Now was his time to grab his life with both hands and wring out every last drop of what he deserved. For the things he had done, for the lives he had ruined or taken, for the sleepless nights this had caused him, this would be a fair price – compensation back-paid and more.

He resolved to repeat the deeds from the night before and await the mermaid's return. He felt confident he could resist the lure of the song and the voice once more; that he could stop in time to not open the door. His will was strong, his resolve resolute. He could do this, night after night if he had to. He would even tie himself to the bed if that was what it took, but he was determined to milk this naïve creature for everything she had. He would have her bringing him the ill-gotten gains of those now sleeping with the fishes again and again until his floorboards strained with the mountains of riches beneath them. He was soon to be rich!

That night, once more the moon rose bright and silver, once more bathing the tropical island paradise below. The palm trees swayed in a gentle offshore breeze and the people slept soundly in their beds. John left the tavern early that night, resisting the urge to brag to the other patrons when they asked why he was leaving so soon. Accusations of him hiding a lover in his cabin were rife, but he cared not. He had business of another kind with a pretty young thing. The journey back home was quicker than before, though he kept one eye on the rippling sea in the bay. He entered his home and, as he had the night before, locked tight the heavy lock on the door. Into his bed he collapsed and, despite his fears and trepidations about what the rest of the night had in store, his eyes swiftly closed and sleep took him.

The air was thick with cannon smoke and the screams of the wounded and dying. John was crouched, hiding behind a large coil of rope used for the anchor when he felt a strong hand grasp his collar and heave him to his feet. Well-worn leather tightly bound around wood and metal was suddenly in his hand, and a hand shoved him forward into the grey murk. Like a phantom rising from a grave, a shape loomed forward. John strained his eyes in the gloom to try and work out if this was friend or foe, but he had no time to make that call. Glinting in the sudden flash of a nearby cannon erupting, a cutlass sliced the air toward the deck. John dived to his left to avoid the blow and the metal weapon landed hard and fast upon the wood below his feet. Without thinking, with no conscious thought from his brain to his muscles, he lifted his cutlass swiftly up towards the forward-leaning torso and drove the point deep between the ribs of the attacking opponent. It was in that moment it was clear who the man was to John: foe. Wearing the colours of the British Navy, this was a crewman from the ship that was attacking John's. They had chased John's ship, William, *captained by the suave and debonair Calico Jack, for many days and had tried to board her under the cover of darkness. Jack's men, though, had proven to be a tough bunch and were now on the verge of victory, but not before John found himself having to run through a few more of the opposing sailors.*

John had never killed a man, nor seen a dead body. Now, as the sun rose in the east and the sea breeze blew away the shroud of naval warfare, John saw the results of his and his crew's handy work. Yes, there were plenty of John's shipmates lying still and unmoving amongst the bodies, but they were outnumbered three to one by the bloodstained blue coats of the British Navy sailors. Next to him John saw, still and stiff as the boards he lay upon, the first man he had ever killed. His face was contorted and frozen in eternal agony. He had felt the cold of the steel pierce his skin and scrape past his rib bone, finding the path of least resistance. It then found the bottom of the man's heart, slicing into the muscle wall, causing blood to erupt like a volcano, sending blood into the chest cavity and oozing out of the wound between the skin and the blade at great pressure. As John pushed the man backwards and retrieved his blade from the clutches of the man's chest, a fountain of claret sprung forth, finding John's face. He hadn't had a chance to wipe it before another enemy sailor was upon him. He fought for his life. It was him or them. He had to do this; he had to. This was the mantra he kept repeating to himself over and over again as he fought on. Only now, with the results of his night's work before him, he really realised what he had done.

After that, the face of his first victim of war haunted him nightly. When he closed his eyes, he was there, that screwed-up face asking him again and again, 'Why?' Then he found it: rum, the cure for all ailments, and plenty of it. Rum settled the mind and dulled the senses. It made the killing easier to do and sleep easier to find. Rum and mead became John's closest of friends, and as the body count increased so too did the empty bottles.

Scrape and slap, scrape and slap. John's eyes opened with much rebellion. His mind wanted to stay in that rum-soaked haze of a dream. Now the worst part was over, he knew the rest was just drink and haze. Scrape and slap, scrape and slap. That noise, oh the noise. What was making that noise…? Like a jack-in-the-box he sprang bolt upright from the waist up. There in the ink of the night, he sat and listened, remembering clearly now what that sound meant. His heart raced and fluttered, thundering through several beats before skipping, over and over. Fear and trepidation were not good for a man of his age. His body, mind and heart were as strong as the oak masts on the ships he called home, once upon a time. But, like the wood that was left unloved and uncared for, he was now gnarled and eaten by the jaws of time. He neglected to soak his organs in nourishment like linseed oil on wood, instead preferring to attempt to pickle them in alcohol such as the specimens within a biologist's lab. This had not worked.

His heart held out, this time. John heard the scrape and slap getting closer and closer as it had the night before. He listened as it stopped at the door. The handle rattled as a cold, white hand held it and tried to open it. A gentle knock followed this and then the voice – that sweet, innocent voice, almost child-like – it came.

'Please, Sir. Me comb, Sir,' the mermaid pleaded as before. 'Sir, did ye get me gift, Sir?' Desperation seeded her voice now more than ever, sprinkled with the hope of a child just before Christmas upon Father Christmas's lap. She seemed certain the sparkling gifts she dredged from the sea would win over the man and he would trade for her comb.

What value, more than the value of that pile of treasure, does that comb have for this weathered old man? she wondered. It meant more to her than anyone else, for to her it was priceless.

The waves crashed above as strange shapes cut through them. The mermaid stayed below, as she always had, for the sun was still shining. Her mother had taught her to stay beneath the waves when the yellow ball was in the sky, and she did as her mother told her. The danger was too great. But this did not stop her sisters from venturing to the surface during the light time. They chased the strange shapes, jumping and splashing alongside them, bringing back stories of strange creatures that walked like sea birds on two legs but looked like merpeople from the waist up. The mermaid's sisters told of how good looking the men on these wave cutters were, and the young mermaid could only dream of what they looked like. She dared not disobey her mother. She was a good girl and did as she was told.

The young mermaid did have leave to explore the seabed, though, far and wide, and took great advantage of this. She delighted in the tropical wonders amongst the seaweed and the kelp beds, within the rocky caves, and she even found old wave cutters lying still on the sea floor. Within them she often found objects that caught the light and sparkled and shone, which she found wondrous and beautiful. She gathered them up and stored them in a nearby cave in secret. But the most precious of all her trinkets was not one she had found, but one she was gifted. To show how much she trusted and loved her, the mermaid's mother gave her the comb, a family heirloom passed down through the generations, used but always kept safe.

Her mother entrusted her with this comb. Then, one night, when the yellow light in the sky had long gone to bed and the fainter silver ball hung in the sky, she finally succumbed to temptation. She swam to the surface in a shallow bay and there, in the light of the silver ball in the sky, she had brushed her hair, feeling for the first time the fresh air on her skin and in her lungs. She realised she was as much at home above the water as below and she liked it. The sound of the waves and the breeze, of the gulls wheeling above her. This was heaven. This was…

Realising at last that she was not getting a response to her pleading and down-hearted her payment was not enough (*Those shiny things obviously were not worth much, then,* she thought) she started, at last, to sing.

What shall we do with a drunken sailor?
What shall we do with a drunken sailor?
What shall we do with a drunken sailor,
If he don't give me comb back?

The words in her sweet voice were like the ringing of the bells of doom to John. Above all else that night, this he feared most. As the melody drifted through the locked door and into his ears, despite his straining of every muscle and sinew as the night before, the same result happened. His legs betrayed him and swung out of bed, and up he rose to his feet. Step by dreaded step he marched against his will to the door.

Pull him down to Davy Jones's locker,
Pull him down to Davy Jones's locker,

He prayed for this torture to stop soon. No amount of treasure could surely be worth this torment, could it? But the money he would have, the mead, the rum! So much rum! But the door was now in front of him and his arm raised up, his hand stretching out.

Pull him down to Davy Jones's locker,
If he don't give me comb back.

As his hand fell upon the key, tendons tightening, ready to turn the key, the singing came to a sudden stop. His hand stopped just as abruptly. He froze, statue-still in the gloom, daring not to move for fear of giving his presence away to the mermaid just inches away from him on the other side of that wooden door. To think that the night before he had wanted more than anything to be with her, to have her, to kiss and hold her, and now her feared her more than death itself. For she was death, the bringing of the end for that old sailor. He was sure the innocence would melt, giving way to rage and anger, if he opened that door. She was, after all, part fish – and fish were unpredictable, skittish.

The mermaid stayed for a moment in the silence of the night, listening to her words being swallowed up by the darkness. The man was surely not at home, she thought, but maybe tomorrow night he would be, and more treasures, no matter how worthless, would surely help buy her most precious of items back before her mother found out. With a heavy heart, she turned and scraped and slapped her way back to the cool waters of the sea to return to her cave.

John, regaining full control of his body and having heard the mermaid leave, turned and returned to his bed. There he wiped his brow with the corner of his blankets. Sweat beaded heavy on his forehead with fear and now the relief of being free once more stemmed the flow. He had to do something different tomorrow. This could not go on.

Half a bottle of rum later sleep arrived, exactly as it always did when it was called by the golden liquor. John, once more, slipped into the dreams of the past that would haunt him until his dying day.

A ship of his own, finally. His rise to captain was soaked in the blood of the enemy and the innocent alike – such was the case for those on the wrong side of the law. As he stood behind the ship's wheel, steering the course and barking the occasional order to the crew (something that led to his raspy voice in later years), John looked out at the islands beyond. These were part of his patch now, and all who sailed on these waters knew it. He had guided his ship and crew around Cape Horn without incident and had charted a course back north, skirting the western edges of the Americas. North of the equator they had headed west even further to a string of islands not yet on any map and unknown to any westerners. It was some years before James Cook would discover these paradises and name them the Sandwich Islands, later to be known as the islands of Hawaii.

John and his crew visited many of the islands and traded with the locals. They exchanged worthless trinkets for finely carved bones, exquisitely crafted wooden weapons, and objects carved out of the finest shells plucked from the bottom of the tropical waters. They would then make the long voyage back to the east coast of America to trade and barter, as well as raid and plunder supplies they needed from other ships foolish enough to sail too close.

John's last name was soon forgotten, for his crew began calling him by another. The locals on those far-off islands would point to him and say, 'Kanaka', which to them meant 'man', but the crew believed it to mean 'leader' or 'captain'. The word was fun to say and to play around with in their mouths and John took a fancy to it. He felt it gave him an air of mystery, so he kept it for his own, from then on only ever being known by this name. Besides, why keep a family name from a family that had used him as a child and never tried to find him after he had been stolen away? Did they even know he had been stolen? Did they even care?

Whilst John was kindly to the simple savages (his words for the native islanders) his ire and anger at the wrongs of his past were clear for all to see when they entered more familiar waters and faced more familiar foes. British, Spanish – they were all the same to John. His cutlass and pistols knew no difference between blue or red; they only saw uniforms and the threat to John's way of life. Blood, smoke, and screams, drowned out by plenty of rum. Day after day, month after month, year after year, trading, selling, stealing, and killing. The cycle went on. Crew members came and went, sometimes voluntarily, sometimes not. It was all the same to John. They either did their job or they helped remove the barnacles from the hull whilst still at sea – a one-time only job.

Consciousness hit like a wave and John sat upright. He rubbed his eyes, yawned and stretched and tried to come alive. Reaching for the bottle by the bed, he realised the rum was gone and he would have to face being sober until he could get to the tavern to buy some more. This saddened him deeply, but he was wrenched out of his slump by the memory of what would be waiting for him outside his door. The spoils of war – the war, not of blade and bullet but of words and willpower – awaited him.

Upon opening his door, he was greeted by a most marvellous site. A pile twice as large as the one from the day before. As with the day before, there was a mix of gold and silver, diamonds and rubies, and precious stones of all colours, cuts and carats, all covered in seaweed, kelp, and a sheen of seawater. John's eyes lit up like a child's on Christmas morning. With great haste, he gathered his ill-gotten gains, removing more of the floorboards to hide the treasures underneath them. With the door now shut but the floorboards still up, the old sea captain looked upon his haul. It was worth more than he'd ever aquired during his time off the west coast, and it was all his. No splitting and sharing it with his crew. He secured the boards back in place. Not that it mattered, John had never had any visitors to his shack, but he erred on the side of caution nevertheless.

His mind now turned to what to do about this troubling mermaid situation. He couldn't go another night without meeting the grisly fate he feared. So, on went his boots and down to the harbour he went, in search of parchment, quill and ink, and a cooking utensil…

The mermaid sat at the bottom of the sea, her mother in front of her, a small rock in her hand. She was teaching her daughter to read. Although the merfolk had little to do with the folk of the land, they had learnt a few things over the years through – often misguided – relationships. These relationships were the reason the mermaid's mother forbade her to go to the surface during the daytime. Her mother, though fearful of the land folk, saw the deciphering of these symbols as important, and the other mermaids agreed, adopting them and the language they were in as their common speech. The mermaid found the understanding of these symbols and their meanings came naturally to her. She excelled in reading and made her mother proud. But as proud as she was now making her mother, she held that secret of her recent night-time activities close to her heart and never let slip for fear of the repercussions.

After a day filled with learning, and an evening of adventures within the caves and coves, the young mermaid saw the silver light was once more out in the sky and knew it was time to go and see if her gifts had been enough this time to recover her comb. Surely twice as much as the night before would secure the exchange, she had thought.

Making sure her parents were asleep, she swam without a sound to the bay. Checking the coast was clear, she heaved and hauled her slender frame onto the shoreline and began clawing at the ground, dragging her body up the path to the cabin. Her tail was perfect for the water, strong and streamlined, giving her great speed and manoeuvrability, letting her keep up with the swiftest of fish such as the graceful marlin – but on land it was no more than a heavy weight to be lugged around. She flapped it furiously though, trying to propel herself further to little effect.

At last, for the third night in a row, she reached the old shack on the hill. She had watched with her keen eyes from the water, two nights prior, as the stumbling man made this very climb and entered this building. She had then followed, but to no avail. This was her last roll of the dice, she thought. If she got no answer tonight, she would return to the sea broken-hearted. The threat within her song wasn't real; she knew that. She would not even hurt a sea slug, let alone drag a man to his death. Her sisters were fiery of temper; they would take revenge if wronged, she was certain of that. But on the whole, they were a peaceful race, acting only with violence when absolutely necessary or when their lives or lives of their loved ones were threatened. No, she would never resort to violence, accepting her fate: her mother's wrath.

Tonight, though, there was something different greeting her at the door of the shack. The treasures had been gathered in, but there was something altogether unfamiliar on the doorstep and a piece of parchment upon the door. She reached up and took the paper. Knowing the symbols – thanks to her mother's teachings – she began to read. Although the letters were scratchy and hard to understand, she slowly and carefully read the note to herself.

John sat in his bed listening. The scrape and slap had roused him and he had spent the time until then praying his plan would work. His ears strained to hear the sound of parchment being torn from a nail before silence fell. Then came the sound of a hollow metal object being lifted off the floor followed by the unsettling and all too familiar scrape and slap, this time vanishing off into the night. The plan had worked. The mermaid was gone! He had mountains of treasure and a large purse of coins gained from the sale of the comb. That night he slept soundly in his bed. More soundly than the past few nights, that was for certain.

Sensing a rising unease upon the seas between the British and the Spanish, John decided in his old age that enough was enough and he would cut his losses, take what was his, and leave the pirate's life behind. He sailed his ship to Panama City, where he bid his ship and crew goodbye. From there he bartered passage across the land to the east coast, where he paid for onward travel to the islands of the Caribbean. There he found the shack he would make his home, purchased it legally, and settled down. This was the first above-board dealings he had made since he was a child selling salted cod in the harbour of Whitby, and even then it was just a cover for the smuggled goods he hid on the cart.

When John awoke the sun was shining. After a life of crime, of robbery and murder, of drink and debauchery, John had done it. He'd escaped the law, earnt his fortune and settled down to drink his life away in peace and tranquillity. He had found his happy ever after, even if, he admitted to himself, he deserved it least of all men in this world.

As John was settling into his new life of ease, the mermaid sat upon a rock somewhere around the coast of the island. The rock was within a large tidal pool that filled with each high tide. She sat, much as she had sat that fateful night in the bay, only this time there was no comb in her hand but a colander. The hole-filled straining implement had been left with a note on the door the previous night and had filled the naïve young mermaid with hope. She knew the place the note had mentioned and had made her way with great haste to the spot and begun to get to work.

It was later that evening, when her mother had not seen her all day, that the mermaid's sisters found her on a high tide. They asked her what she was doing and she simply showed them the letter before carrying on with her task. The other mermaids read it slowly and with much horror. It read:

Mermaid,

Forgive my tardiness in not returning the comb that clearly means so much to thee. The gifts which you have bestowed upon me show that you are agreeable to a fair trade. I have a task in need of completion. Your assistance in this task I consider to be fair exchange for your comb.

You may know of a pool around the coastline that sits on its own at low tide but returns to the sea at the high tide. I am in need of your assistance to bail out the pool using the tool I have provided before the next high tide. If you fail, then you must try again, and again, until the task is completed. This will solve a very large problem I have and, in return, to show my gratitude, I will return your most precious of combs.

Yours faithfully,
The Sailor

The older mermaids saw through this deception immediately. They knew this was an impossible task. There was no way in all the seven seas the young mermaid would be able to bail out the pool in one tidal cycle with a bowl full of holes. It emptied as quickly as she could throw the water away. They begged and pleaded for her to stop, but she cited the letter and the promise that if she did this, she would get her precious comb back. She also made her sisters swear to secrecy with regards her mother. She said their mother must never know that she lost her comb, for she feared what her mother might do.

The sun shone hot during the day – so hot it blistered and burnt the poor, delicate skin of the young mermaid, for it was not used to direct sunlight and had no protection like the darker-skinned people who lived in the air. And these days were many and long in which she toiled. The nights came, cooler than the days; a lot cooler. The wind changed and brought a chill upon it during the nights, freezing the never-stopping figure upon that rock. With the burning and the freezing and not a drop of water touching it for days, nay weeks, the mermaid's skin cracked open. The scales on her once beautiful tail shrivelled up and fell like autumn leaves, floating out to sea. But still the mermaid stayed at her fruitless task and still her sisters called for her to stop... until one day, all of a sudden, she did. She curled up on that rock and her eyes closed. The colander slipped from her fingers and sank to the bottom of the tidal pool, where it lay for many a year. Crabs and molluscs made it their home, seaweeds and anemones clinging to it, fusing it to the rocks with the coral, growing through the holes and anchoring it firm, until it became as much a part of the sea as the rocks beside it. And there she lay, a creature of the sea, dead in the air above. An unnatural death for such a wondrous thing.

Her sisters found her soon and carried her body down to the bottom of the sea. The water was cool and soothing on her skin, but she had no life left in her to feel it. Her sisters piled the stones and shells on the sea floor high over their beloved's body, leaving holes for the fish and other sea creatures to enter and dispose of the remains, such was the way of the sea. The merfolk understood that all things come to an end, and they then become life for other creatures, and so it goes round and round, ever and always.

The merfolk mourned, but none more so than the mermaid's mother, who finally heard the full story after the burial. She grieved hard and fumed so the water boiled around her. The merfolk feared to go near her for the best part of a week until her anger had cooled and a clear head had returned to her. And with the return of a clear head came the want and need for vengeance. The merfolk had slept for too long; ignored the atrocities the menfolk on their wave cutters had done to them over the years. This was the final straw, the end of the line for their patience and tolerance. This poor young mermaid, so innocent and true, had been taken from them in the most cruel and deceptive way and there needed to be vengeance. The council of merfolk met three weeks after the death of the mermaid and they spoke long over what course of action was best. It was decided that for too long they had done nothing, so now they would use their gift to exact revenge upon the men of the land. They sent word to all corners of the seven seas, to all merfolk alike. The message was simple. They were to use their song to lure the menfolk to rocks, causing them to dash their wave cutters upon them. And then, when they were weak and vulnerable, splashing around, defenceless, the mermaids were to drag them down to the ocean floor, to Davy Jones's locker. The water would force out the air from their lungs and with it the life from their body. They agreed they must wreak revenge on the cruel man that had killed their sister, however, they knew not who this was, as the letter was signed simply 'The Sailor'. So, they simply took revenge on all sailors, regardless of colour or creed. By drowning all sailors, they hoped to get the one sailor responsible for this crime.

And so it was, through his thoughtless actions, John Kanaka, former fisherman, smuggler, pirate, captain, now a rich drunkard, brought about the death of tens of thousands of sailors around the world. His happily ever after caused immeasurable pain, torment, and upset. Mermaids were no longer a good omen, a thing to watch on in wonder and delight for the sailors, but a portent of doom. Their siren songs signalled the end for all those who heard it, with only a handful ever escaping to tell their tale. Mermaids became an evil menace, previously fondly remembered in children's fairy stories, but now the subject of the horror stories shared around the fire in taverns by the sea across the globe in a thousand languages, both in tales and songs.

T'was Friday morn when we set sail,
And we were not far from the land,
When the captain, he spied a lovely mermaid,
With a comb and a glass in her hand
O the ocean's waves will roll,
And the stormy winds will blow,
While we poor sailors go skipping to the top,
And the landlubbers lie down below (below, below),
And the landlubbers lie down below,
Then up spoke the captain of our gallant ship,
And a brave old man was he,
He said, 'This fishy mermaid has warned me of our doom:
We shall sink to the bottom of the sea!'
O the ocean's waves will roll,
And the stormy winds will blow,
While we poor sailors go skipping to the top,

And the landlubbers lie down below (below, below),
And the landlubbers lie down below,
Then three times around went our gallant ship,
And three times around went she.
Three times around went our gallant ship
And she sank to the bottom of the sea.